The Smallest People Alive

The Smallest People Alive

Keith Banner

Carnegie Mellon University Press
2004

9/04 16.95

ACKNOWLEDGMENTS

"*Is This Thing On?*" was originally in <u>Washington Square</u>,
"*The Doll the Fire Made*" in <u>Harrington's Gay Fiction Quarterly</u>,
"*The Wedding of Tom to Tom*" in <u>Full Frontal Fiction: Best of Nerve</u>,
"*The One I Remember*" in <u>Kenyon Review</u>,
"*Where You Live*" in <u>James White Review</u>,
"*Spider in the Snow*" in <u>Witness</u>,
"*Holding Hands for Safety*" in <u>Men on Men 6: Best Gay Fiction</u>,
"*The Smallest People Alive*" in <u>Kenyon Review</u>, and
"*Lex*" first appeared on the Internet magazine, <u>Nerve</u>.
"The Smallest People Alive" also appeared in the <u>O. Henry Prize Stories 2000</u>.

Book Design: Philip A. Stephenson
Cover Design: Grinning Moon Creative

Library of Congress Control Number: 2003112694
ISBN: 0-88748-426-3

10 9 8 7 6 5 4 3 2 1

Contents

"If you look a dog in the eye too intently,
it may recite an astounding poem to you."

--Jean Genet,
Funeral Rites

Is This Thing On?

1

This is Shorty, coming at you over Psychic Radio USA.

This is me, live, in the living room of my girlfriend's house. Ladonna Wickersham is her name, and her foot has been cut off for diabetical reasons. I myself have an oxygen tube going up my nose.

This happens to be my everyday existence. I sit here, and I watch Ladonna sit there.

"Shorty," says Ladonna right now, opening her eyes. "I feel hungry for something sweet. Can you believe that?" Her face is lit up all of a sudden, thinking of sweets. She has a pretty smile. On TV is that Santa Claus movie she always watches after the soaps go off.

"You want me to get up and get you something?" I say.

Her hair is the color of leaves that are about to turn to dust on the sidewalk. Her complexion is rainy sky. That leg ain't the end of it. Gangrene goes up, not down. The walls around her glow from the pink light of the TV. Santa Claus is flying over the sleeping city.

"Do you mind?" she asks.

After finagling with my oxygen tube, I go and open the fridge door. I called the exterminator day before Ladonna got out of the hospital. Figured that would be a nice gift for her. But now the little fuckers are back, crawling down under the crisper, probably a whole society in where the lettuce goes. I grab Ladonna a little thing of chocolate pudding, and for myself cold pizza from the other night.

Me and Ladonna eat. Keep on with Santa Claus the

Movie. Ladonna takes her spoon and scrapes the sides of
the disposable cup, making the sound of a mouse getting
in through a wall.

Hoyt, Ladonna's borderline-retarded son, comes crashing
in a few minutes later, with Tanya, his jail-bait girlfriend.
Tanya's got on her short-shorts and a tight little T-shirt in
the middle of October. Hoyt with his buck teeth, broken
glasses that he's fixed with silver duct-tape, unwashed
Denny's uniform.

"What you guys watching?" Hoyt asks.

"Santa Claus," says Ladonna.

"Hoyt, get the hell out the way, son. I can't see through
you to the TV," I say.

Tanya looks cross. Don't you let him treat you that way,
Hoyt, I hear her thoughts say.

Hoyt moves toward his mom's leg-stump. He touches
the drain-off bag like it's some delicate pet. Caresses
the long tube going from the stump to the bag, then
accidentally kicks it with his heel.

"Goddam, Hoyt, be fucking careful," I say.

Tanya comes over, stands by her man. She ain't right in
the head. I know that for real. Inside her head is a drawer
of dirty clothes: dark, damp, but pretty clothes.

"Shorty, back off," Hoyt says, not looking at me.

I reach over the end table, seeing some cockroaches
scatter by the lamp. Grab my cigarettes and my lighter,
take the oxygen out of my nose and turn the nozzle
down. It is dangerous to be smoking around oxygen, I
know, but you got to do what you got to do.

"I got to work tonight," Hoyt says.

"Again?" his mom says.

"Yeah."

"I'm going with him!" Tanya says.

Ladonna laughs, "I thought that manager told you she couldn't go to work with you."

"He did but they're desperate. So I told him if she can't come, I ain't coming in, and he said okay as long as she stays in the backroom." Hoyt looks proud that he was able to work that out. I have seen the inside of Hoyt's brain also. It's the attic of a new house built on the cheap. Completely empty, with that brand-new house smell.

"You are gonna lose that job, son," I say.

He still doesn't look at me. "Quit calling me son," he says. Tanya strokes the boy's shiny hair. Ladonna closes her eyes, her face gently frog-like from hospital fat.

I pick up the oxygen hose now, turn it on. They all like me to do this. I turn on the oxygen, let it hiss out from the end of the hose, squeezing the tip. Then I take my lit cigarette to the tip. Like magic, a perfect blue ball of pure flame hovers at the end of the hose, the size of a baseball. It stays there for as long as I let it. If I was to stop squeezing the tip, the fire would back up into the belly of the tank and explode, killing all four of us. I bet they don't know that part. They just watch the ball. It sedates the room. Finally I turn it off, smoke some more. On TV, Santa slips down the chimney to put presents under some lucky stiff's tree.

Hoyt gets up and kisses his mom, thinking: I love you, Mom, and I hope you never die.

"I'll see you in the morning," Ladonna says, mouth closed up against the pain of everything. Inside of Ladonna's head is like the inside of that couch she is

sitting on, dark and musty but soft with a wood spine,
little creatures scurrying to and fro, also some spare change
that's fallen out of people's pockets.

Hoyt and Tanya leave without saying anything else.
Hoyt is staying over at Tanya's house, as he doesn't like to
be around Ladonna when she's this bad. The two of them
have set up house in her dirty pink little-girl bedroom.
Her parents don't seem to care. Probably on crack, or
maybe deranged alcoholics.

Ladonna gets some shut-eye. So I go back into the
radio-studio in my head. I flick a control-switch in my
own head, going: Hello? Hello? Anybody out there? Is
this thing on?

2

Thanks for returning my call.

Sure. Sure. I understand completely. That's what I
was telling Ladonna over there just yesterday. I said,
"Never give up the hope." I didn't. Now look. I'm a
bonafide psychic.

Now when I was a little kid, I used to do this sort of
thing. In the back of a tore-up pick-up truck in my
uncle's yard. They thought I was a dwarf. Some smart
doctor broke both my legs when I was 9, to stretch them
out. He said he might put goddamn pins in, but he died
a month later of a stroke, and that was that.

So that summer I had two casts on. My uncle takes
me out to the truck and makes me a bed out there in the

fresh, country sunshine. My uncle never got married, by the way. He was like a priest, except he devoted his life to wayward animals, not God. He had a damn zoo in his backyard. I don't know where he got the dollars to feed them broken-legged foxes, blind raccoons, the squirrel with the half-cut-off head from being under the lawnmower. One time, my uncle even had a mountain lion, big old bobcat, half its face blown off by some poacher's shot. He nursed Old Bobcat back to good health, needle-and-threading its face into a constant smile. But I'll tell you what. That animal loved him.

Anyway, there I was, nine years old, with my broke legs in the back of a pick-up. I think I may have been speaking to you, or perhaps one of your co-workers. Hell maybe even your daddy. Sent out messages to wherever, nothing else to do. I got back one message, I remember. The voice was pretty garbled. Bad reception, I guess. Never figured out what it was saying. But I knew it was especially for me.

That was not a real conversation back then. I was just a kid. This thing here, this conversation we are engaged in, seems to be different. Is it not? More of a back and forth.

Hey, wait a minute. Look over there at Ladonna. You think she's breathing?

3

"Stop poking me."
"You looked like you were dead, honey," I tell her.

"I feel worse than dead," she says.

"You want some diet pop?"

"No."

I sit back down. Reinstall my oxygen tube. All I hear right now inside my psychic head is a hung up phone.

"Shorty," says Ladonna, *The Young and Breathless* going off.

"What darling?" says myself.

"Would you put in Santa Claus?" Her baby-sick voice.

I laugh. "Why are you so loving of Santa?" I ask, getting up, a tad bit woozy. "I mean, honey, it ain't even Halloween till next week."

"Because." Little baby-doll, sick-girl voice. "Cause. I like Christmas, and it's sweet. Santa Claus. Remember when you dressed up that one time?"

"Why, yes I do," and I have to smile. I dressed like Mr. Claus when Ladonna was working at the nursing home, goddam, eight or nine years back. Got the Santa suit at K-Mart, walked into the dining room. Just a few of the old ones gave a shit, eating their blendered-up meals. Me, I went loud as joy can go: "Ho, ho, ho! Merry Christmas, folks!"

Laughing and jolly, I carried a sack of orange slices and paperback romances and aftershave, all of which Ladonna had wrapped in pretty paper. She worked cleaning rooms, but had to quit three years back due to her declining health.

But back then, as I ho-ho-ho'ed my lily-white ass off, the old fucks did not really care. Now I have to tell you that hurt, that feeling like no matter what you do for people, they will always want to finish eating first.

"Christmas," Ladonna goes now. She looks up at me, almost like she is pleading, her eyes tearing up, then the pain passes through her, and she closes her eyes again. "I got to sleep," she whispers. "I got to. But go ahead and put the movie in."

4

Sometimes I see me and my uncle in my head, driving off. Me in the front-seat with my double-broke legs, and him tall and faceless, driving. Old Bobcat is in the backseat, because it likes to go for rides too. It is summer, dark and hot. There is no sound as we pull into a drive-in theater that looks closed down.

We park, my uncle clipping the speaker onto the window. A movie is already in progress up on the screen. Nobody else is here, don't look like. I have my broke legs stretched across the seat. Old Bobcat purrs in back.

The movie is like nothing I have ever seen before. This movie has me in a Santa Claus suit in it, holding a gun up to Ladonna's head as she lays butterball-naked on the couch. Naked, asleep, moaning from pain. Me as Santa pulls the trigger. Ladonna's head blows off onto the couch, through the back, onto the wall.

After undoing that itchy fake beard, I turn the gun toward my own mouth.

My uncle is watching, even though his eyes look like shut-off lights. He does not seem to like it. How many animals has he had to put to sleep? I wonder. The ones that can't pick themselves up and eat, the ones who get mean and start howling non-stop.

Old Bobcat purrs now, on its back in the backseat, its face in that surgically stretched smile. Bobcat wants to play, kicking up his hind legs.

I hear the second shot, but don't look.

5

Somewhere around in there, Hoyt and Tanya come back.

"Guess what?" Hoyt asks his mom. Tanya stays in the doorway. They are dressed like they were the other day. Denny's uniform, short-shorts and t-shirt, only Tanya now has a rag-tag coat over her little fashion ensemble.

Ladonna whispers, "What?" Her eyes open like daybreak on a rainy morning.

"Me and Tanya got invited to a Halloween party!" He grins great big, like this is the answer to all his problems. He pushes his broke glasses back up his nose.

"That's nice," Ladonna says from her prone position.

"It's this guy I work with," Hoyt explains, serious.

"We think he's a queer," says Tanya. "But that's okay, cause he has a big house." She giggles into her hands.

Hoyt looks at me from over there beside his mom. "She okay?" he whispers.

I stand up. Can't see nothing for a sec. "She's your mom. You tell me," I whisper.

Hoyt doesn't say nothing. I put on my shoes, grab my keys, go out, brushing past Tanya. She grunts and calls me a name, tells me I smell bad.

Same to you, sweetheart, I radio her, as my mouth is currently involved in a little bit of a coughing fit.

6

Are you back?

Gets pretty boring talking at myself. One thing though: try to warn me. I'm driving here. Yeah, this is the Cadillac. My only souvenir from my life of crime. I'll have it stuffed and put in a museum like Trigger.

This is the street old Kent lives on. Pretty bad, ain't it? Urban blight. Wish my oxygen tank had wheels. I walk on up to Kent's front door with a bright green, cardboard skeleton hanging on it.

Knock, knock.

"Shorty," goes Kent's voice behind the door, after he has peaked out through the curtains. He has to use a walker from the brain damage he got after being shot in the head. His house smells like an animal den. Kent clangs his walker back past the foyer, which is where he is throwing all of his garbage instead of taking it out to the curb.

He looks back at me, as I kick some egg-shells out of my path. He has a pink towel on his head after taking his shower. One time, me and Kent, we almost killed this kid who robbed one of our trucks, and that was when Kent here could fucking run. He chased that kid down, dropped him. We beat on him pretty good. We were just the paid help, two-bit nobodies, but that kid fucking with our truck, there was no way.

"Shorty, you look like 100%, Grade-A compost."

"Yeah, well, same to you, buddy."

Kent's face as he laughs is not right. It's like he is afraid once he stops laughing he is going to have to go ahead and die.

"Hey Kent, I need me a gun," I say, grinning.

"What kind?" he says.

"Oh just a little nothing hand-gun, whatever you got."

He gets up. The towel drops onto the floor off his head. He has black dyed hair, and the inside of the pink towel is just covered in black goo. He walks with his walker over to a lopsided book shelf. Points at a tackle box. "Grab that," he says.

Inside this tackle box are four or five little guns. I grab the one I want, hold it.

"There's bullets in a plastic baggie there," Kent says, now back over in his La-Z-Boy.

I get some. Used to have four or five guns at the house. Ladonna made me sell them all. She said it was dangerous, especially with Hoyt being borderline retarded and so much in love.

I put it in my coat pocket, hold onto it there, then let go. It drags my coat down on that side. "Kent," I say. "How much do I owe you, sir?"

I look up, and Kent might be having a seizure of some kind. He is sitting there like a zombie shaking, eyes opened a little but not enough to signify nothing.

Kent old friend! I do that one psychically, trying to shake his spinal cord. I then latch onto his thoughts.

Suddenly, I am in a place with strobe-lights and storm
clouds and spinning tires, mixed up with the quiet of
drowning. Angels start blowing kisses, the way fish
breath underwater.

I pull back out of the psychic world, exhausted. Kent
is still there before me. He shakes bad, but it looks like
he likes that.

I leave with the gun and the bullets.

Thank you, Kent, thank you buddy.

7

My uncle once said:

"All the animals in the woods are a part of what makes
you a human being. All the sounds they make, all the shit
they shit, and the blood they do bleed. Buddy boy, you
listen to me. All the broken bones and the ripped fur, and
all the fear that makes them wild. That is you, and what
you think, and it is the only thing that is true."

That's what he said right before he shot a German
Shepard dog that got rabid. It got quiet, and its eyes rolled
back into its head right before the shot, like it knew.

You don't care about that, now do you? You need
this to be over. You need to get a move on, don't you?
Angel of Mercy? Is that your name? Or Astronaut?
Little Green Man from Mars? Holy Ghost?

You don't have to answer. You're busy, I'm sure.

8

There is Hoyt, and there is Tanya. Bride and Groom for Halloween.

Ladonna is only smiling.

"This is my mom's dress," Tanya says. She whirls around in the living room. Hoyt got a tuxedo at Goodwill for three dollars, he says. He models around too.

"Three dollars for that?" I say, wheezing, oxygen back in my nose.

Hoyt says, "That's cheap, Shorty." Almost completely outraged.

Ladonna says to Tanya, "Come here, little girl."

Tanya goes over, bends down. Ladonna, with what strength she has got left, fixes that veil. Places it centered on Tanya's ratted hair.

"There," whispers Ladonna. "You two go on, and have a nice time." Her face is blank with pure pain.

Hoyt and Tanya stand together in the doorway, the threshold. They are waving. Then they are whooshed off in a ball of blue flame out of here, as I stand up. A blue globe of fire called The Rest of their Natural Lives.

9

Breaker, breaker 1-9.

This is me putting bullets in the gun in the kitchen. Ladonna asks me for something sweet right then. I put the gun down on the counter. Grab a little thing of chocolate pudding, brushing a cockroach off the top. I go out, give it to her. But she has already fallen to sleep.

I stand there. I watch her.

As I take off all her clothes, she whispers, "Oh, Shorty. I can't do nothing sex-like now. Everything hurts, honey. Oh Lord. Watch out for the drain-tube, Shorty, honey."

She falls back to sleep once I got her naked. I stand above her, and I picture that hand-gun there in the kitchen, like an angel on the counter, black and heavy for its size, but angelic anyway. Then I get a mental picture of the Santa Claus suit up in the attic, boxed up with the beard. We keep everything up there. It's a fire hazard and a half.

"Santa Claus the Movie," my Ladonna whispers in the nude.

She has curled up into a fetus-type position. Seems to be floating up, even as she sinks deeper into the couch. Maybe she's ready. Yes I think she is.

The Doll The Fire Made

Other than the vomit I just now cleaned up, the wedding and the party after have turned out to be a well-organized affair. Darlene and Edgar are the newlyweds — her third, his first. Edgar and myself go way back, to say the least.

I bump into Hunter, Darlene's boy, inside the church reception-hall's kitchen. Skinny and pale, his dark hair styled back with mousse, he stumbles towards me as I throw the paper-towels I used into the trash.

"Hey thanks, Don," Hunter says.

"For what?"

"Man, I did that." He walks to the doorway and points down the hall where the vomit had been. His three-piece suit is way too big on him, and seems to be in the process of swallowing him whole.

"How old are you anyway, kiddo?" I ask.

"Fourteen," he says, grinning, despite it all.

"Fourteen," I go, whistling comically. "Drinking will stunt your growth." I grin right back at him, go and sit him down in a folding chair. Hunter puts his elbows on his lap, his face in his hands, like The Thinker. I go over and wash my hands in extra-hot water. There's a little window above the sink that shows the left side of the reception-hall. Someone has put on Bob Seger's "Hollywood Nights." None of us go to this church presently, but Darlene did at one time, and that's how the whole thing wound up being here. A few people dance to Bob Seger on the concrete floor out there. Standing beside the table of unwrapped gifts, Darlene has long dark hair, wearing a lavender dress. Right next to her is Edgar, short, half-way bald with a goatee around his mouth, in a nice new suit we got him at Sear's.

Edgar spots Hunter sitting in the kitchen right then, like he'd been looking for him a while. He walks on back. It was probably Edgar who gave Hunter the booze. Obviously, being in a church, this is a no-alcohol gathering. Edgar, being Edgar, however, always has some on him.

I turn around from the sink.

"How's it going boys?" Edgar says, going on past me.

"Fine," I say.

Edgar laughs loudly, walking toward Hunter. "You look like crap," Edgar tells him, almost in a whisper.

"Thanks a lot, Dad," Hunter goes, saying "Dad" sarcastically, but then smiling.

"You're welcome, Son," Edgar says back.

Hunter gets up and pukes a little more into the trash-can. As Hunter wretches, Edgar puts his hand on the boy's neck and massages it, saying, "You'll learn." Finally Hunter stops. Edgar looks up at me, "He'll learn, won't he?"

I nod my head, trying to smile. Edgar goes past me, saying, "Better get back out there."

Once Hunter leaves to go lay down somewhere, I go

out and take a few after-dinner mints from a dish on a table, pop them into my mouth. Darlene and Edgar are dancing to "We've Got Tonight."

This is when I want to kill both of them, at that moment. Of course, I had felt that feeling all through this whole event. It flashed on and off, like the oil light in my car, this desire to bust out of my kneeling-down-and-wiping-up-the-vomit self, just to bust out of it all like the monster I possibly could allow myself to be. I could even tell Edgar what it was like. That's the crazy thing. I could say, "Edgar you ass-hole, you mother-fucking ass-hole. Edgar how can you do this to me?" He would take all I said in, and try to be understanding. I had said all that stuff several times in fits of midnight rage, around the time he first mentioned marrying Darlene. At that point, I thought he was simply toying with me, like he did a lot, trying to make me jealous.

Edgar had said, as I was his best-man and I was with him out there in the red-plush-carpeted foyer right before the music started earlier today, "Don, I know what it took for you to be here today, and let me tell you — I am just blown away."

I could not talk. For a second, I felt like I was glowing like a religious figure, or extraterrestrial.

I go over to Edgar and Darlene right after "We've Got Tonight." Five or six people are still hanging around the food-table. The newlyweds both look at me, bright-eyed.

"Thanks for everything," Edgar says.

Darlene whispers, getting close to me, smelling of lilac perfume:"I know how hard this was for you, bud." Her mouth is caved-in slightly from extensive dental work, but she's pretty, I have to admit, for her age, which is 42. Both Edgar and I are pushing 40. Before she and Edgar even thought about getting hitched, Darlene knew about Edgar and myself, and it was okay, she said. She had no problem forgiving Edgar's past as a bi. She even liked me. She said it was time, though, for both of us to grow up.

"I wish Edna could have been here," Edgar says. Edna is my mom who I live with, Edgar used to live with. It's a running joke, how their names are so much alike.

"That flu won't quit," I say, my teeth grinding. We don't move or speak, no eye contact, but then after a second or so, I look at Edgar, smiling without opening my lips.

"Nice suit. Where'd you get it, Sears?" I say. They both laugh at my joke, out of relief. I walk back into the kitchen to find something else to do.

By the end of the evening, Hunter has fallen to sleep on the floor by the gift-table.

"Get up you little alkie," Darlene says, trying to tie Hunter's shoes. She looks up at me, "I swear, he can't keep his shoes tied for nothing."

I look at Hunter's face right then, beautiful, smooth, in a little pain, but also trouble-free, as Darlene finishes tying

his laces. Edgar comes over with his Polaroid and snaps
Darlene and Hunter's picture, laughing.

"You guys ready?" Edgar softly kicks Hunter's calf with
his toe. "Come on you little runt." Slowly, Hunter obeys,
complaining about his head. I walk out with them to the
parking lot. Hunter gets in the back-seat of Darlene's
Nissan and collapses.

"Are you gonna go back and clean up in there?" Edgar
asks me, after shutting the door on Darlene's side. "I mean
you realize you don't have to, I hope."

"Yeah, I realize that." I look down at the ground. I will
get over this feeling eventually just by sweating it out, but
right now I am here with him, sharing the same space.
We'd been boyfriend-boyfriend for close to four years.
The desire to kiss him on the mouth is still inside me, like
I'm constantly trying to swallow a pill that's way too big.

Edgar comes closer, and I freeze.

"You'll find someone," he whispers, serious as a heart-
attack.

"You're just too nice of a guy not to." Edgar walks to
his side of the car then. The gravel under his feet makes
the sound of old bones coming apart.

I get home around eleven. Mom has already gone to
bed, but the light is on in her room off the kitchen. Edgar
and I had once shared the master-bedroom, as Mom
turned the room downstairs into hers. It was too hard on
her "Liz Taylor hip" to go up and down all the time. I go
toward her room, but right when I am almost at her door

I hear a crashing sound in the basement. I walk down, and the washing machine's jumping all over the concrete floor. I run to it and unplug the thing. Open up the lid to find all our silverware in a gray sudsy soup, some of it bent beyond repair. I go back up and pound on Mom's door. It swings open. She is sitting up in her bed, staring right at me.

"What did you do?" I ask.

"What?" she whispers, her hair messed up and sweaty.

"Mom, you tried to wash silverware in the washing machine," I say. "Why would you do that? It's all torn up now."

For a minute, she does not get who I am. Thankfully, it snaps into place. "Now what?" she asks.

I go over and feel her forehead. Not really that hot. It's probably not the flu anymore. Confused, she is still looking at me. Then she relaxes back into the bed. Closes her eyes and asks: "Did his wedding go okay?"

"Yeah." I flick off the light-switch. She didn't want to go anyway. She had always liked having us both around. It made her younger, Edgar and me pretending we were boys, in a way. Boys in junior high staying all night with each other all the time. Sometimes we would make S-mores and watch movies till the sun came up, or go fishing at odd hours at the pay lake in Trenton, or laugh obnoxiously at the stupidest things on earth.

She drops back to sleep. I figure I'll just let the silverware incident go.

As soon as I turn away from her, the door-bell goes off.

I run and flick on the porch-lights. Hunter, Edgar, and Darlene, all still in the same clothes from the wedding, are on my stoop. I open the door.

"Our apartment building burned down," Hunter says, no longer hangover-looking. "Turn on your TV," he says, excited.

We all go over to the living room, sit down. I click it on to the news.

"Hopefully it hasn't already come on," Darlene says.

I look at Edgar. "What in the heck?" I ask.

"Our apartment building burned down, Don, swear to God," Edgar says, looking like he's been electrocuted.

"We went back to change and drop Hunter off? Well, we pull into the apartment complex, and there are fire trucks everywhere. We go to ours, and it's just all gone. Just this pile of hot ashes," Darlene says. Her face is hollow-looking, her hair put up now in a pony-tail. I notice how her lavender shoes are covered in black dust. Edgar's hands are covered too.

"Our whole building was torched," Hunter says, lit up from seeing it. Tragedy, to someone his age, is not tragic. It's got a special glamor, like you can start all over.

"Everything is gone man," he says. "I lost my boom-box and CDs. Thank God most of my good clothes are still at my real dad's house in Texas."

The news has gone into a commercial.

"God," Edgar says, smiling a little. "The reporters there had a billion questions. We got to be the center of attention. I mean by the time we got there the fire was almost out anyways. The reporters were just about to do their stories, and they kind of clung onto us. You know, the wedding-night angle."

Darlene laughs like all this just has to be funny or her head might explode. We laugh along with her, but we stop when the story appears on the TV. On the screen, Edgar and Darlene have microphones shoved into their faces.

"A wedding and a fire, in the same night," Darlene says into one microphone. "Talk about a roller coaster ride for your emotions."

The reporter sends it back to the news-room right after Darlene says that. I hear Mom mumbling in her bedroom, so I have to excuse myself.

"What's going on?" Mom says from her bed.

"Edgar and Darlene's apartment burned down," I say.

"I thought they got married tonight," she says.

"They did, but their apartment burned down too."

Suddenly Edgar is behind me, smelling of char and Brut. He puts his hand on my back, but I move away, even though in that moment of touching I feel hopeful and alive all over again. He goes in and sits next to Mom on the bed.

"Edna, can me and Darlene and Hunter stay here? Our apartment burned down. We were gonna go to Gatlinburg for our honeymoon, but now we don't have anything to wear or anything."

Amazingly, Edgar is laughing about it.

"Now what?" Mom says.

"Edgar. She's really sick. I'm sure it's okay if you stay here. Right Mom?"

"Sure," Mom says, then rolls over toward the wall. Edgar cranes his neck to see me, his eyes wide and dumb and awe-struck.

"You must be the kindest man on earth," he says.

The TV is off, the ash-tray full, we have eaten a delivered pizza. Darlene gets up and stretches. "I need to take a shower. You mind?" she goes.

"Not at all. Mom has a night-gown you can wear," I say.

"Thanks," Darlene whispers.

I go and quietly retrieve a pink flannel nightgown, walk upstairs and put it on the little table outside the bathroom door, knocking and telling Darlene. When I go back down, I see Hunter and Edgar looking at each other, just sitting there and looking at each other on my couch. I get a strong feeling in the pit of my stomach. As I go closer, I see that Edgar is whispering stuff to Hunter.

"Hey," Edgar says, looking up, stopping the whispering. Hunter looks back at me, and I see his face, white as a sheet, very beautiful because he looks excited and scared like an animal.

I break them up with:

"Well, Hunter, you can sleep on the couch or on a sleeping-bag, and I can sleep on the couch. Because I'm giving the bed upstairs to your mom and her husband." Like a security guard, I am standing right in front of them.

"Couch is fine," he says.

Edgar looks up at me, like he's sorry again. I ignore him.

"The couch it is," I say. I stomp back upstairs to get blankets. I feel like I am ready to lose it finally, but then on my way into the bedroom, I hear Darlene in the shower, singing. She has a beautiful voice, surprisingly, singing "The Rose," that Bette Middler song. I stand there, right by the bathroom door, caught up in it. Then Darlene just stops. She shuts the water off, and that's when I hear her start to sob. I don't move a muscle, listening. Darlene quits after about thirty seconds, though, and then I hear her start to sing again as she dries herself off. I go get the blankets, leaving her alone.

Edgar and Darlene spend the night of their honeymoon in the bed Edgar and myself used to have relations in. That's the way it is. Nothing to do about it, but put my sleeping bag and blankets down onto the floor beside the couch.

Hunter says, sitting on the couch, in the dark, "I can't sleep."

"I bet you can't," I say, looking up at the ceiling. I shouldn't be mad at Hunter because Edgar is trying to seduce him. I mean, the kid is not all that bright anyway--he's in some slow classes at school, Darlene said. I shouldn't blame Hunter, no. I should call the authorities and get Edgar for child-molestation and maybe even

Darlene for neglect — at least that's what I am thinking
right now. Or just kick them all out. Be done with it.
Instead, I try to calm myself by gazing up at the water
stains on the ceiling, in the shapes of dragons and Model-
T Fords. I think back to Mom putting silverware in the
washing machine. I see her, flushed and confused, doing
that. Maybe a smile on her face.

The only light is the glow coming in from the street-
lamp. Hunter does not have his shirt on. He has a boy's
chest, skinny with ribs glowing through.   On his left
shoulder is a tattoo of a skull with wings his dad got him
last summer.

"So are you gonna miss Edgar?" Hunter asks me.

"Yes," I say.

"He's a nice guy." He does not make eye contact,
smoothing his hair back.

Right then, I picture all of Hunter's clothes on fire.
In my room, Darlene and Edgar are holding onto each
other, I bet: the fire has made their honeymoon more
meaningful. It's like they are clinging to each other to
make the whole thing make sense. As if the reason the
apartment burned up was so that they could enjoy their
new life together more.

Hunter steps over me to go pee. I get up and sit on the
couch, finding the warmth Hunter just left.

When he comes back, Hunter asks me, "You want to
switch?"

All the sacrifices I have made, being the best-man
and cleaning up after people and grinning and bearing

all of it, all that suddenly goes up in flames, replaced by
the feeling that finally what I want has come to me, out
of nowhere. The fire makes sense that way. I deserve
something, after all.

I look up at Hunter, and he is looking back at me. He
repeats, "You want me to sleep down here?"

I nod, "No, no, I'll sleep down there." But I do not get
up. I smile, patting the cushion next to me. Hunter looks
at me, kind of irritated, kind of confused, but then he
comes and sits down, quiet. Without his approval, I kiss
him. He flinches.

"Hey," Hunter says. But he does not move. I feel like
I have magic powers suddenly, like my eyes are emitting
freeze-rays. I grab his hands and kiss him harder on the
mouth, so hard he seems to know he can't get away. I lick
his lips and chin. He makes me stop by standing up. He
says something I don't hear.

I go down and lay on the floor, like an emotionally
wounded German Shepherd. I realize what Hunter said
was, "Where's the remote?" A few seconds later, he finds
the remote, and the TV comes to life — an infomercial
about special non-stick pots and pans. We don't say
another word.

Next day, Mom is surrounded in smoke in the kitchen.
Despite not feeling good, she got up at the crack of dawn,
to make breakfast for all of us. That's the kind of lady she
is. She has on her maroon housecoat, her pink slippers.
Anytime she cooks anything now, there's a big smog.

"Where's all the silverware?" she asks, not remembering.

I don't feel like telling her. I'm in my robe too, and I know I must look pretty pathetic with my knobby knees.

"Well?" Mom says. Her face registers bewilderment, then snaps back.

"Don't worry about it. I'll get it."

I go downstairs and grab up all of the wet silverware and put it in an old plastic bucket, walk it back up and clean it in the sink, throwing out the bent pieces. Mom is too smoke-surrounded to notice. Edgar is up now too, in a pair of jeans and sweatshirt, standing on the other side of the stove. He flicks on the exhaust fan, then rubs his hands together, like a lumberjack, not really noticing what I'm doing.

"God I'm famished," he says.

Mom ignores him, trying to get everything ready. I put the silverware into the dish-drainer, and Edgar says to Mom, "Listen Edna, let's not get into it, okay? I don't think I can take your cold-shoulder treatment right now." His smile is like a high-school senior's, arrogantly full of itself, but stupid enough to be innocent.

Mom looks at him through the smoke, nodding her head, laughing, "I'm just fixing you your breakfast."

We all eat and finish quickly. Mom outdid herself, but now she looks exhausted all over again.

"My goodness," Mom pronounces all of a sudden, getting up. She looks around at the four of us and seems to forget where she is again. "Goodness," she repeats, then walks slowly back to her room, shutting the door, like that might be the only answer.

Stacking plates, Darlene goes, "I feel like I'm getting something too. They say stress can help bring it on." She grabs Edgar's hand and puts it on her forehead, smiling. "Am I running a fever?"

Edgar whistles, "Yep. This is one hot momma right here." He pulls her down onto his lap, looking at Hunter. Darlene leans back, forcing a giggle, her long hair touching the floor.

"I thought we'd go over there today," Edgar says to Hunter, Darlene getting up. "Go out and see if there's anything left."

"Yeah that's great," Hunter says. He gets up and walks into the living room, flicks on the TV.

Taking plates into the kitchen, Darlene says, "Why don't you guys go and then maybe I can go tomorrow? I just don't feel like seeing it." She starts running water, squeezing an almost-empty bottle of Dawn.

I look at Hunter in the living room as he wraps an afghan around his shoulders like an Indian chief. He looks up at Edgar who is sipping his coffee at the table, all master-of-the-universe-like. Showing off for Hunter. A huge burst of pure hate shatters what calm I have going. I want to take that cup of coffee out of Edgar's hand and fling it at the wall. I want Hunter to see me do that. I want it to register in both Hunter's and Edgar's minds that I mean business.

Instead I pick up the rest of the dirty plates from the table. Take them into the kitchen, where Darlene is doing dishes, her eyes half-closed. She opens them all the way once I come in.

"How do you replace baby pictures?" she asks me, her hands in the water still.

I wonder if that's a rhetorical question, but I go ahead and say, "Do you have the negatives?"

"No," Darlene replies. She starts placing the dirty plates into the dish-water, not saying anything.

"That's a real shame," I say.

Their building is the only one that burned down, as the fire department did a good job containing the blaze. It is just a big mound of black ashes with little flecks of color and half-burned things you have to get up on to see. On this bright cool sunny day, people are already going through the rubble.

We get out of my car. Edgar and Hunter walk side by side, but then Hunter breaks into a run, and Edgar looks back at me, "Neat kid."

His eyes sparkle, as though he understands his smile is torturing me, as though he understands I know what he is doing with Hunter and with Darlene both. I wish he had been burned alive in the fire, but he is beautiful still. I think back to one time before all this, way back when we first started to sleep together, how one time we went out to play pool, and he started coming onto the waitress at the bar where we were. It wasn't Darlene this time, but somebody else. I found that to be a kind of turn-on, to tell the truth. Edgar acting, well trying to act manly. And

the waitress says to him and me both, "Aren't you two
— you know?"

She just knew. You could tell, maybe by the way I
looked at him. The waitress wasn't being mean. Edgar
said, none-the-less, "You are one cold and ugly bitch."

We had to leave. We went back to the house, and he did
it to me. After he was done, Edgar said, "You like this way
too much." He was smiling, but there was horror in his
face. "I mean you are way way way too into this."

"So?" I said, grinning at him out of love and desire,
grinning too because I had scared him.

"So don't."

"Don't what?"

Edgar got out of bed, naked, went across the room
to get his pajamas back on, like if he remained naked
something bad might happen.

"Don't moan like that."

I laughed, starting to imitate the way I moan during
sex. But I stopped. Even then I knew this would not last
forever, this love. I figured eventually I would just have
to extinguish this love I had for Edgar, like a cigarette. It
has turned out not to be like just one cigarette, however.
Sadly enough, it has turned out to be more like the whole
habit of smoking.

An old man in a flannel shirt, work-pants and baseball
cap is pulling a scorched bicycle from the ashes. Edgar
and I walk on over to him, while Hunter rushes to where
their apartment used to exist.

"The whole thing just collapsed fifteen minutes after

the fire started," the old man says, like he's the tour-
guide. "I mean, just that short of a time and space. It was
amazing." He spits out some tobacco-juice.

"You know how it started?" Edgar asks, squinting his
eyes.

"They think — well Edgar you remember that blind
hippie lived down in the basement by the washers and
dryers? Well they think it started in his place. He might
have threw away some incense or something while it was
still burning. He got out alive, thank God, but that's what
they're saying."

"Good Lord," Edgar says, "I would hate to have that
on my conscience." Edgar and the old guy get into a
conversation about possible class-action law-suits.

I go over to where Hunter is, passing a woman who has
found a dresser in a pile of ashes. She opens a drawer, and
the clothes inside are perfectly okay, except they probably
stink. Over on the other side, a young couple are pulling
a baby-bed out from under a collapsed beam.

Hunter yells my name. I run over, out of breath.
Hunter has crazy eyes, standing above something. I go
over and see that it's a curio cabinet on its backside. I
remember it. Darlene kept her collection of antique dolls
in it in the living room. Some of the dolls are out on
the ground, in mint condition, not even charred in the
slightest way. Perfect in their old-timey clothes, gleaming
white in the sunshine, against the black of ashes. But on
the other side of these dolls is a mound of doll-flesh, those
dolls burned up into each other, arms and legs attached by

scorched plastic like scar tissue — heads half-melted, eyes staring out of plastic guck, hardened overnight. The good dolls are right next to the burned ones.

Hunter looks up. "That's a souvenir," he says, pointing at the melted doll thing. "That right there is the goddamn mother-fucking souvenir of the year!"

Monday, next day, two of my employees don't show. The janitorial service I work for is doing the telephone company offices downtown. If people don't show up for their shifts, I, being the on-site manager, get stuck doing the job. God knows no other employee will be kind enough to offer, and I'm too afraid to tell them to do anything extra anyway. They get paid crap wages. Being demanding will only make them quit sooner.

I have to do floors 14 and 17. Plus all my management duties of making sure everything my employees did is kosher. Office-people are really particular about what janitors do to their buildings at night.

Anyway, I'm on 14 and vacuuming. It's a long wide-open office sectioned with gray cubicles, like a honeycomb. Inside each cubicle is a desk and phone and filing cabinet. As I vacuum, I pass framed pictures of families and jars of candy and notepads in the shape of Snoopy and Garfield. I'm proficient at vacuuming of course, a real pro, even getting behind desks and chairs, methodical. Right when I am almost done, the vacuum gives out, however. I turn it over and try to see what's wrong, but it's not detectable that way. I unhook the bag to find out it isn't the bag, which is only half-full.

Then I start dismantling the machine itself.

All I'm thinking about is getting done, checking out my employees, going home to face Darlene and Hunter and Edgar and Mom, all of it a stew of names and faces and emotions, like my damn head is a crock-pot that's been kept "on" all day. Suddenly I look down on the beige carpet, and I see that I have taken the whole vacuum cleaner apart. Little black rubber-belts and coils and pieces I don't know from where, like I have discovered vacuum cleaners have skeletons now. I look down at all that, not knowing how I am going to put it back together. I feel lost then. A little panicky and lost.

Time for a break, obviously.

I go out, get some coffee out of the machine. The area by the elevators is quiet. I remember I am all alone up here. I peer out the window beside the coffee machine. Up 14 stories, you can see all the other downtown buildings, glassy skyscrapers, the sun setting in downtown Dayton. There is stirring magic at this time of the day, seen only by janitors, I guess: all the glass of all the buildings lit up like that, pure and orange, like a calling.

Hunter and I try to clean those dolls from the fire in the kitchen, after I get off work. Darlene doesn't really care. I mean she cares, but is too tired and stressed out to worry about her antique doll collection too much.

For some reason, though, Hunter and I care very much. We give the ones who didn't get burned baths. They still stink bad, even after the bath. We hand-wash their outfits too.

In the living room, Edgar is laughing at us, but also saying snide things, obviously jealous that we have this little project together.

"Look at those two playing with their dollies," Edgar says. Nobody laughs. I feel sorry for him, and I go ahead and laugh, saying, "Ha ha very funny. Keep the jokes coming out there." Mom is in the living room too, with them. It is around 10 PM. They are watching a movie Edgar rented.

Hunter and I came up with idea yesterday of selling them at the flea-market with a sign that says, "THESE DOLLS SURVIVED AN INFERNO." I look at Hunter as we clean them now. He is trying real hard to get a doll's arm into a dress shrunk from washing. His tongue is halfway out. All of a sudden, I want to protect him. I don't know from what. From Edgar, from myself? From alcohol? From fire? When I peek out into the living room, I see Mom still has that completely confused expression, propped up in her chair, like Queen of the Scarecrows. Darlene is braiding her own hair, her eyes shut down. I look over at Edgar, and he says something else smart-alecky. I wonder when he is going to just get up and come into the kitchen, to put a stop to this.

On the floor beside the trash is that one big doll the fire made: six different scorched and melted arms and torsos and legs, crystal eyes shining, heat-bubbles and black pieces too. A doll lasagna. Hunter is going to save it, his one and only souvenir.

I go up to him as he tries to fix the doll's arm through. I push him slowly up against the fridge, out of view of the living room. I kiss his mouth, deep. He acts like I have just tried to drown him. But he does not scream.

"Hey what's going on in there?" Edgar says, getting up from the recliner.

"Let's try to get this done," Hunter whispers, pushing away from me. He is talking about the dolls.

I nod my head, breathless, feeling stupid. Scared of myself, of what I can do when I set my mind to it. Scared of myself, but nobody else.

The Wedding of Tom to Tom

The first time I saw the two of them doing something
was also the first night I worked alone at the place. I was
nervous from the start, and the woman on before me was
a total alkie. As soon as I got there and clocked in down
in the basement, she went, "They're all in bed and they
got all their pills."

Then she was gone. I guess she walked off the face of
the earth, because she didn't come back the next night,
when she was due on. Never called or anything.

Anyway, I was walking up and down the hall of the old
house after she left, nervous, like I should be checking
on something. It felt like a haunted house, but I felt I
belonged, like I was a ghost but didn't know I was yet. I
could hear the retarded people, all five of them, snoring
and tossing and turning. Sleep's never been so loud.
Then I heard real intense moans coming out of the back
bedroom. They didn't sound like they were from sleeping
people at all.

I went to the door at the end. It had this great big
poster on it of Michael Jordan shooting a basketball
through outer space. The door was halfway open.
Suddenly, the moaning became like some weird song.
Like singing and going crazy at the same time. I slid the
door open the rest of the way, thinking about somebody
maybe having a seizure. I'd just seen the training video

on that the other day at my orientation. They had this dramatization about a woman dying from drowning on her own vomit while having a seizure. God knows I didn't want that my first night. I'd made a decision from the get-go: I am keeping this job, no matter what. I was gonna stop living like trash.

I opened the door, turned on the lights.

Tom B. was on his knees in front of Tom A. They were both naked and very white. I didn't know either of them too well at this time, so I just stood there. Tom B. is skinny and short, and Tom A. is big-bellied with short legs and no butt. Both are about middle-aged or older. Tom B. has a burr cut, and Tom A. has curly dark hair.

So there they were, like that. Blow-job position.

I wanted to scream or laugh or cry, all at the same time. This was my first night alone remember. I figured they shouldn't be doing that, but I didn't know what else to do, so I shut the door back, like a maid in a sitcom catching people in the middle of something.

Of course I forgot to turn off the lights. I was getting ready to open the door and turn them off when I saw that one of the Toms had already got it. Almost as soon as it was dark in there again, they were making that same crazy silly sex music.

I went back to the living room. I lit up a cigarette, wondering if I should call somebody. Kate Anderson-Malloy, the home manager, told me when I saw that video the other day that if I had any questions just to beep her. "Just beep me," she'd almost yelled, smiling like a whack-o left in charge, but you had to respect her enthusiasm.

I could still hear them. I smoked real deep and seriously contemplated just walking off. Not beeping anybody, just going. Two retarded men participating in a blow-job. I mean, I'm not some Pollyanna by any means. But yes it shook me the hell up.

I was about to go back there again, stupidly afraid that maybe Tom B. might get choked or something, I was on my way, when I heard footsteps. I stopped right toward the third bedroom, and I saw Tom B., back in his pjs, tiptoeing back to his room. He had this serious face on in the emergency-exit-sign light. Half-demonic, half-angelic, but dramatic, like he had gone off and now he was returning from his journey filled with beautiful new things to tell. I felt sorry for him sort of. I heard him close his door real careful. Heard the rest of them continue with their loud, gurgled sleep.

Sleep deprivation, and witnessing a retarded blow-job, made me feel kind of paranoid that whole damn night. I kept smoking cigarette after cigarette. Kate Anderson-Malloy had told me at orientation that sometimes state people come out to check on group-homes in the middle of the night, to make sure the staff they're paying for aren't getting paid for sleeping on the job. I kept seeing headlights scatter across walls all night.

Plus there was my whole ex-boyfriend thing brewing too. I was being stalked, so to speak. He didn't know it, but his ass would soon be in jail. Anyway, to keep myself

busy I started snooping through the filing cabinets over by
where the scales are, near the door to the basement, this
little makeshift office there.

I got out Tom A. and Tom B.'s files. I read Tom B.'s
first. It said right at the start that Tom B. suffered
from moderate mental retardation and also possible
schizophrenia. He could talk but had trouble with his
speech. He had lived his whole life in some institution
in Columbus, Orient Institution, but was sent here when
it closed down, as was Tom A. In fact, at that place,
according to Tom B.'s file, both Toms had a reputation for
being "obsessed with each other's presences" so much that
they often had to be split up and put into separate parts of
the institution. Usually, though, according to typewritten
reports in the file, they found their way back to each
other. Tom A. could not talk, and was more retarded than
Tom B., so his file was pretty skimpy, except I read one
part where when he was four years old his step-dad burnt
him with cigars.

By that next morning, which was a Saturday, I knew
the whole damn story by heart. Since no one had to go
to the sheltered workshop, Kate Anderson-Malloy had
written me a note in the log that they all could sleep in
till 8. I made a big breakfast, to let them know I was an
okay chick. I mean, the works. Now that I'm a full-time
shift-supervisor, lead direct care in fact, I just put the boxes
of cereal and gallons of milk and they go at it. But my
first time, I made waffles and heated up the syrup in the
microwave, had some sausage patties that I also miked.

Full glasses of juice and paper napkins, picnic-type dinette table set like the Waltons were about to come down and eat. It was ready around 7:45 that morning, and no one was up, so I got antsy and went down the hall again, the warden who makes breakfast.

When I woke up Tom A., he looked at me like the way — I'm sorry this sounds pretty awful — like the way my cat does. Lonesome inside, without the capability to explain, and yet also relieved that he was off the hook from having to tell me anything. In fact he smiled at me, and I said, "Why aren't you chipper?"

I almost added, as a joke, "Looks like you got you some last night."

But I didn't.

He sat up. His belly hung down quite a bit. He had a boyish face though. I noticed on his back all those cigar scars. He walked over to me and put his hand out, like a gentlemen in a silent movie.

I shook it. He let out this huge scream that about killed my ears.

"Thanks," I said.

I went and got Sally, this little woman with Down's Syndrome who may have had Alzheimers too. She was in her pink bedroom because that's the way her sister painted it for her. She had on a pink flannel nightgown and looked like a melted doll in a playhouse in her canopy bed.

I got Damon, black guy with a big head that had water inside it. He had a pump installed in his skull that kept the water from drowning out his brain. I knew all this stuff from Kate Anderson-Malloy and from the files. I knew Damon used to live with his prostitute mother and she used to sell him out to freaks. He was very quiet and could only say, "Mona Lisa."

Got Larry up. He talked too much. Soon as he was up, he started gabbing.

"Hello. You're new here. You're name is what? May I ask what?"

His eyes were open great big. He was sitting on a rocking chair in his room with posters of big-breasted women black-electrical-taped to his walls. Tall and bony with a big bald head and very red lips.

"Anita," I said.

"We ain't going out anywhere today," he said, looking out the window. You could totally tell he hated going outside.

"Okay," I said. "I made breakfast for you."

He turned his head toward me and clapped his hands in an exaggerated, almost sarcastic way, but his voice seemed for-real. "How nice," he said. "Don't smoke around me. I have asthma."

I said okay.

Tom B. was the last one, as his room was at the end. There was Michael Jordan staring at me. His door opened as soon as I got there, and he was in a pair of dress pants and wrinkled mint-green dress shirt, feet in brown vinyl slippers. He looked uptight and yet really wanting to please. His eyes still had sleep in them. I saw him from last night, naked, going down on Tom A.

"Breakfast is ready," I said.

"Tanks," he said. Speech impediment.

"You're welcome."

His smile was unnerving, shaky around the edges, and it almost made me angry at him.

"Tanks berry much," he said and then started walking toward the kitchen.

I followed behind him. All of the retarded people were seated at the picnic table now, and the shock on all their faces almost made me bust out crying. It was like Thanksgiving with breakfast food. I know I'm sounding like some sentimental idiot, so I won't go on, but they really loved what I'd done, and it had been a while since I got that kind of reaction from anybody.

"Look at dis Tommy," Tom B. said to Tom A. "Look what she did fow us."

Tom A. smiled bigger. He grabbed his fork in one hand and his knife in the other, like any minute, any minute.

"Mona Lisa," Damon said, his voice very low. "Mona. Lisa."

My relief came in at eleven. She seemed a little drunk too. A lot of drunks work in group-homes, like it's their way of paying penance: a vodka binge, then they go in and wipe up retard's ass and they think they don't have to quit drinking. But this woman, named Raquel, could be drunk but it didn't seem obnoxious, even at eleven in the A.M.

Right when Raquel walked in and went down to the
basement to clock in was when Archie called me, my
drug-dealing ex-fiancee. This job was sort of my antidote
to all I had just gone through with him, kinda like I was
paying penance too but just for being a total fucking
fool. But Archie kept following me. I mean, I was living
with my dad, and I was moving all my stuff out of the
townhouse we were at one time sharing, and every time I
went to get more stuff he was there, hang-dog in the face.
Sometimes when I was going around doing my business
and shit I would see him in his Escort in the rearview
mirror with that same hang-dog, stalker look. Like he was
having his picture taken for the cover of Pathetic Small
Town Dope Dealer Magazine.

"What? How did you get this number you son of a
bitch?" I was whispering, but still I hoped Raquel did
not hear. Everyone was out in the living room, watching
VH1, doing whatever. Tom A. and Tom B. were sitting on
the love-seat, of course. Holding hands. Sally was in her
pink sweat suit, on the floor, talking to a piece of a jigsaw
puzzle. Larry was really the only one watching the TV,
while Damon rocked in his lounger with his eyes closed
kind of like Stevie Wonder does.

"I hired a private detective," Archie said. He laughed.

"Bull shit. Listen, I'm at my new job, and I am trying to
make something outta myself."

"Okay, okay."

"So it's over."

"I love you so much."

"Go smoke your crack, Archie. Just fucking go smoke your crack."

I hung up. As if she'd been waiting at the bottom of the stairs for me to finish, Raquel marched up, her hair all ratty-looking, in a pair of nylon sweats and flannel shirt. She smelled like perfume and cigarettes and just the thinnest vapor of Jack Daniels, almost sweeter-smelling than the perfume.

"Hey," she said, not looking at me.

I had just finished up with the kitchen, so I was ready to go. Pulling an eleven to eleven was more than I thought it would be.

Raquel looked out in the living room. Then she got panicked sort of. She turned around and told me, "You're letting Tom and Tom sit out there like that?"

She kind of laughed.

"Yeah," I said.

"Good God, if Kate found out...."

Raquel yelled, "Tom. Hey Tom. Don't hold Tommy's hand now. You guys split up. It's time for some alone time. Okay?" Raquel's smile was nervous, like she was talking to someone during a hostage crisis.

Tom B. looked up, responding to being called Tom. He smiled. But his eyes were afraid at the same time. He blew out a sigh and let go of Tom A.'s hand and stood up and went over beside Sally on the floor, small and polite like a little Japanese guy.

Raquel turned to me, "If you let them do that, they don't know when to stop. They'll get so into each other they'll not know when to quit. One time they locked themselves in the bathroom for a day and all they did was — well — you don't want to know. Let's just say they went through a whole bottle of hand lotion." Raquel laughed into her hand. She flopped down at the picnic-type table, lit up a cigarette.

I smiled. Sally was talking to Tom A.'s foot now. I wondered just what the fuck I was getting myself into. Heard Archie's voice in my head, pleading. At one time, he was gonna do construction and I was gonna go back to community college for something in nursing. Ha.

"Guess I'll go," I said.

"Yeah," Raquel said, smoking.

She stood up, and with her cigarette dangling walked out into the living room.

"Look at all my babies," she said kind of loud, but then she looked up at me and her eyes were real clear. They were the eyes of a drunk lady who used to have kids but for some reason lost them and now she was in a roomful of retarded people that she was claiming as her own, and she was saying it like a joke on herself, on the retards and on me. But it wasn't meanspirited. It was pathetic and it was sweet.

I laughed a lot right then. Probably from being so sleep-stunted. Tom A. and Tom B. were trying to sneak off for a quickie right then, and I saw. So did Raquel, squatting next to big-headed Damon, grabbing two throw pillows from the couch and tossing them at both Toms, hard.

"Stop right there." Her voice was joking and not.

They stopped, went to separate corners like obedient prize-fighters. I wanted to give them permission right then. Go for it. I wanted to get the hell out of there worse though.

I left that day without saying anything else. Thinking I was not ever going back.

Time sure flies when you're having so much fun. So to speak. I mean it really does. That was about a year ago, all that I just explained. Of course I went back for my next shift. Actually, if I remember correctly, I got called in to cover the other drunk lady's shift, the one who never came back.

Now Racquel and me go out and get drinks together all the time. I am on my way to becoming a drunk-lady direct care worker myself. Raquel and me practically run the place.

Some things, even with time, don't change, however.

"You want to get together?" It is Archie. He just got out of jail last week. I'm standing in my dad's house right now, and can hear Dad out in the garage sawing on something.

"Good God," I say, and I laugh because Archie's voice sounds so familiar and yet shocking, like a CD you think is fucked up and you press play and it's not.

"It's me."

"You were up for six years."

"Time out for good behavior. Plus Johnson County

ain't got no room, and it was my first offense."

He laughs, smoky-voiced. I can picture him, going bald
but with a rugged face and skin color like dank wood.
And his mouth, I always can remember that fondly. Big-
lipped and smiling with strong white teeth. He is so into
dental hygiene.

Dad comes in sweaty, mouthing, "Who is it?"

I just roll my eyes. "Listen, I gotta go."

I hang up, and Dad looks at me, "Archie."

"How'd you know?"

"You had that look. He calling from jail?"

Dad is washing his hands in the sink, over all the dirty
dishes. He is a tall guy with freshly cut hair. He goes to
the barber three times a month. On disability because of
his back, so it's about the only place to go during the day,
outside of his old work site and I think they might have
told him to leave he was going there so much. Now he
spends his time out in his garage/workshop making things
like a vacuum cleaner with a digital display. Inventions he
hopes to patent. He takes a lot of pills for pain.

"No. He's out."

Dad dries his hands on paper-towels.

"Wow," he says. "You know what, I had a vision."

Dad thinks he's psychic. He even has a license to be a
practicing one and goes to psychic fairs in Cincinnati and
Dayton. Even has business cards: ROLAND SIMMONS,
L.S.P. (Licensed Spiritualist Practitioner). With that
license, he can legally marry people. He's marrying Tom
A. and Tom B. tonight, in fact. Not legally, but still.

"You did?" I say.

"Yeah. I didn't want to say nothing." His eyes go so sincere, like Bill Clinton, when he talks psychic talk. It's a sad yet joyous thing, his psychic powers. Like a person who can't read suddenly being able to. The psychic stuff is one of the primary reasons Mom dumped him though.

Dad looks at me with big puffy Darvon eyes. "But I saw you and Archie together in a motel room."

He laughs but stops.

"Thanks Dad. There is no way."

I go into the living room. I've straightened it up for the wedding tonight. It's all planned. Me and Racquel planned it. I have white and sky blue streamers and I made a cake and punch. Dad's technological shit is still everywhere in piles, cables and old TVs and VCRs and computer monitors and stuff, but I scooted all of it around to make it look like an aisle. At first, we were gonna rent a hall, but that would have drawn attention to it. This is sort of a secret operation of course. If Kate knew, or if Tom A.'s brother, his legal guardian, knew, we'd all be fired, possibly up for charges or something.

"Think about the headlines, Anita," Raquel said one night at Applebee's after work, over cocktails and cigarettes. "Two Group-home Workers Force Clients into Homosexual Marriage." We got tickled and started making up juicier and juicier ones, ending with: "Shot Gun Homosexual Retarded Marriage Performed by Crazed Psychic while Group Home Workers Get Drunk and Laugh Their Asses Off."

Anyway, Tom A. is being made to move, or at least that's the threat. Kate Anderson-Malloy caught them one morning doing it in the bathroom about four months back, and since then she's been on a campaign, although she's just totally professional about it. At a staff meeting, where all of us gather at the main office in McCordsville, Kate, kind of flabby with really nice hair and an excellent pant-suit, got into a sort of tirade. I mean, she's a bitch, like most managers afraid of doing any real work are, but also there's this weird, loud lovingness in her face as she pronounces her proclamations, like against her compassionate instincts she's always having to tell us these things. And so she looked at all of us in the paneled conference room, and she went:

"Look. We have tried everything with those two. I mean, I'm not against love. I'm not against human sexuality. I'm against obsession. Those two are obsessed. I mean. I talked to Mr. Allen, Tom A.'s guardian last night on the phone, and he told me they've been like that since Orient, since they were boys, and it's hard to stop that kind of behavior. I mean, you can't. So we're just gonna move Tom A. over to Franklin Street and move Juanita from other there to our place. Juanita's real cute. You guys are gonna love her. I mean, Tom A. and Tom B. can still see each other, but supervised. I mean, what I'm afraid of is that they are gonna end up hurting each other. Physically. There's all kinds of issues here. I mean when I walked in on them the other morning, Tom A., excuse me, but Tom A. was anally penetrating Tom B."

The way she said "penetrating," I had to laugh. Racquel looked over at me, and our eyes kind of got conspiratorial.

When Kate looked at me, she had to laugh too. I mean it was funny. Eric, another guy who works with us, laughed, and then all the people, mostly new hires, well we all got the giggles until finally Kate had to stop.

"I know, I know," she said. "This is the people business, and yes the people business can be pretty funny. But let's just try to make this happen smoothly okay?"

Then it got quiet, like we were all suddenly little kids and Kate Anderson-Malloy was the teacher.

Dad's standing at the podium he made for the wedding now. It is in front of the living room window where the TV used to be. He looks kind of dumb, standing there, politician-dumb, like he is thinking how to talk about a big issue in little-people language for the masses.

But I love him. One of his visions about me, and he usually has them after eating late at night, one of his visions about me is that I am going to be famous somehow. He sees me getting an award on a show.

Now he says, making sure the hair he combs over his bald spot is still in place, "So I'm just gonna treat these two like man and wife."

"That's what we want," I say.

The phone rings again, and we let the machine get it. It's Archie's voice. He's singing this Boys II Men song I used to really like, "The End of the Road." It kills me, and I get embarrassed, Dad standing there, smiling.

"What a singer," Dad says.

Archie stops then, and the answering machine has that hang-up dial-tone sound for a sec. I get closer to the podium, pretending like I'm one of the Toms so I can see what it looks like. Dad's eyes go serious. He says, "So this is the wedding of Tom A. to Tom B." He's reading it off an index card. Practicing. What a perfectionist.

"Ladies and gentleman, I now pronounce them Tom and Tom," he says.

The plan was secretly hatched in the basement by the time-clock. Racquel was taking a drink from her Super-America mug, filled with vodka and red-pop. One time she offered me a sip and I took it and boy was it vodka and red pop.

Anyway, it was the evening right after the staff meeting where Kate told us Tom A. was gonna have to move. We were both kind of bummed, and Racquel said, "You know, all Tom B. has ever talked about was getting married to him. I think that is so sweet." She took a big drink.

The dryer was going. Big industrial one for all the piss-soaked bed-sheets and other assorted piss-soaked items. I knew that already, about them wanting to get married. Not only because Tom A. had a stack of old-timey bridal magazines, worn out from looking at them, stacked in his room, but Tom B. and I had gotten into many discussions about marriage too. By this time, we were pretty good friends. Tom A. was more aloof, could not talk remember,

but Tom B. let you know he was proud of what he and
Tom A. had accomplished: 24 years of staying together,
and when Orient shut down and they were going to be
moved out, he knew Tom and him would be in the same
group-home because, "It went alphabetic. So I knew. It
was luck. It was God too. Tink about it, Anita. Tom A.
and Tom B."

It made sense, didn't it? His face, as I was trying to
do my paperwork, was sincere and stupid and scary and
beautiful. You can't say no to that. Well maybe other
people can, but people like me can't.

By the way, Tom B and me never did talk about me
seeing them that first night I worked there, them doing
the nasty, but I'm sure he would have just laughed it off
like nothing. Raquel said they used to line people up at
Orient in the shower-room forty at a time and tell them
to hold their noses and spray them down with a gigantic
fire hose, and then say, "Now soap up," and forty men
would soap up real quick, and then get sprayed again and
some people, the people who worked there, would laugh
as they sprayed them.

So Racquel said that night with the dryer going, "Let's
let them get married."

She looked at me like we were both out of our minds.
Even though she was a lifer, she was also pretty much
timid and obedient, scared of Kate Anderson-Malloy and
not just because she had two last names. But because
Kate had sense to everything she said. Obviously it
made a lot of sense to move them away from each other.

Because they were getting worse. They weren't going
to workshop some mornings, clinging to each other
nude in one bedroom or the other. Other times too, like
they were losing their fear, like they were getting brave.
Helping them to get married would only make them
braver, wouldn't it though? And it definitely would not
stop them from having to move away from each other.

   But Raquel took a big gulp from her vodka and red
pop and she swallowed and she said, "Maybe if they get
married it won't be so bad that they can't live together.
Like Dolly Parton and her husband."

   I smiled. That did not make any sense, but it seemed
right.

   Raquel is already at the group home when I pull
up. She had already helped pudgy Tom A. into his suit.
It's a mint-green leisure suit, from when he got de-
institutionalized, and they gave all them new clothes, back
in the late seventies. It barely fits, and he looks like some
tourist-guy having nerve problems on vacation. Raquel
and he are sitting on the couch, and Damon and Sally and
Larry the big mouth are all in the living room.

   I step in. Eric is in the back with Tom A.

   "He's showing Tom how to shave good," Raquel says.

   Larry asks, "Are we going anywhere? We're not going
anywhere are we?" He's got that totally freaked out look
on his face.

   "No. Just me and Raquel and Tom A. and Tom B.," I
say.

"Thank the Lord. I am just so tired, Anita," he says. He was raised by two aunts in a mansion, kept a secret there with them for years and that's his personality: old-lady stubbornness and laziness and gentility. He relaxes now, secure that he can stay that way.

Sally comes over, spit dripping down onto her pink shirt. Her face has a sweet and scary emptiness to it. She is walking around without knowing anything but with her eyes wide open.

"Pop," she whispers. "Pop, candy. Pop. Candy."

She has gone into this repressed memory thing, where she is always thinking she's brushed her teeth real good and now she deserved some pop and candy. That's the way they used to get her to brush them.

"I don't have any honey," I say.

Raquel, dressed in a long jean skirt and a beautiful orange blouse, her ratty hair pulled back into a bun, gets up and gets some Tictacs out of her purse, "Here."

Sally seems happy, and sits on the arm of Damon's lounger. He pushes her off, saying what he says: "Mona Lisa."

Sally flops down and grunts and kind of laughs.

Then Tom B. comes out with Eric, slump-shouldered high school dropout who wants to be a chef. He has one of those sad mustaches that are barely there. But Tom B. is perfectly clean shaven, in a navy blue suit, black shoes. Handsome, I think.

Eric looks scared, "You guys if anybody finds out."

Larry comes in, "We ain't going anywhere."

"I know, Larry. Calm down," Eric says. He starts to
whisper, "I told Tom that he can't say nothing, and he
agreed, right Tom?"

Tom B. nods, "Right. I won't." He shakes his head
real hard, and goes over to Tom A. He gives his hand to
Tom A. and Tom A. looks dumbfounded for a sec. He
is realizing they are actually going somewhere to get
married. It does not make sense to him, as it probably
doesn't to the people out there reading this, but still it's
exciting to him.

"Come on," Tom B. says, "Come on Tommy."

They're two boys going to church. Two kids, it seems
like. True love does that to you.

Raquel opens the door. They walk out. I look at Eric,
who still is worried.

"God if anybody finds out," he says.

I just go on out.

Thinking: well it's me and Archie in my head, if you
want to know the truth. Raquel's car is bigger, so we
go in hers, both Toms in back, holding hands, just any
regular evening. It's dark and chilly and the headlights
shine on piles of silver gravel. I need a cigarette. I think
about Archie's voice on the phone. Pathetic but rich with
feeling, and I think about the way he would look coming
out of the shower, naked, and anybody naked looks like
they did when they were kids, even with hair and flab
and all the years added on. Something about being
dripping wet and shivering and clean: that's what a kid is.
I remember loving Archie when he was wet and naked.

Pretending not to see him, but he was showing off, even with his rotten body. Coming over to me while I was trying to read course descriptions.

"Baby," he said.

"You are getting water all over the fucking floor."

He laughed. It was all I could do not to laugh with him. Maybe he was on crack right then, for all I know, because he kept all that hidden from me. In fact, maybe the crack was buried when he saw me. Put away in the chest of drawers in his head, and this was love, without crack and without any lies and without his petty-assed, trashy ways.

Maybe, maybe not.

I see them back there in the rearview. Tom A. and Tom B. Looking straight ahead.

"Tanks you guys," Tom B. says.

Dad awaits. So do Raquel's two friends, drag queens that go to her AA meetings. They are dressed conservatively, like ladies who go out to lunch but who also might have some mental health issues. Big, big hair, and they sit on my dad's couch, my dad offering them punch or something stronger.

"Punch. That sounds so innocent and sweet," one drag queen says. Right when we came in, Raquel introduced us. This one is Mimi. The other's name is Salsa.

"This whole thing is sweet," Salsa says.

I smile, and Dad goes to get the punch, and on his way he stops by and pats both Toms on the back. They are standing near a little table of gifts. As Dad pats them, though, his face goes white as a sheet. He almost falls down and has to go over to a dinette chair, panting real bad. The Toms and Raquel all look scared, but I focus on my dad, as Mimi and Salsa march over, Mimi saying she used to work in hospital and knows CPR.

But Dad is not having a heart attack I don't think. His face is pale but not pained.

"Wow," he whispers to me.

"What?"

"When I touched those two," he says.

"Tom and Tom?"

"Yeah." He laughs. People are leaning into us, and I kind of nicely push them back.

"What?" I say.

"I saw this airplane hangar. You know. Great big corrugated-metal, big as hell, and it had this red, well this pink and red light. And I was at one end of it," Dad says, and he sits up, and I back away and all the others stand, listening. It's suddenly quiet as hell.

"I was in this hanger, at one end, it was empty, and just that pink and red light. Like you know there was a fire somewhere. Then I heard this stampede coming from the other side. I swear to God. That was strong, people. Wow." He laughs some more, and Mimi goes, "You psychic honey?"

"Yes I am," Dad says. He looks up proudly, his bottom lip shaking like he might start crying. He's always been emotional.

"He's got a license," I say, to back him up.

"Wow," Mimi says, looking over at Raquel, like thank you for bringing us here. "Well kiss my hand tell me what I want for Christmas." Mimi and Salsa laugh real loud, but Dad just stands up and walks over to the podium.

"Bring them over now. It's time," he tells Raquel, and Raquel brings Tom and Tom over in front of the podium. I run over to the lights and flick switches to make it more intimate, turn on low music.

"This big hangar building," Dad says, from the podium. Tom and Tom are right there in front of him. "Pink light like exploding roses. The red light district. Ha ha. No. A stampede. You gotta hear it. A thousand-plus feet. I am on the other side and I look up and all these shaved-headed people are running right at me in the red light. It's like they just got freed, you know? Like the concentration camp just opened its doors and they got out and they're running. They don't know where they're going or nothing. They're coming right at me. And I want that to happen. I want them to run me over."

My dad is smiling with glassy eyes.

"I want them to run me over," he says, looking right at Tom A. and Tom B. "And they do. They stomp all over me. They gotta get somewhere don't they?"

He's asking the Toms, and Tom B. goes, "Yes."

"They gotta get somewhere," my dad says, and he closes his eyes. Then he opens them real quick.

"That's love," he says.

After taking a sip from her punch, which she had to go

get herself, Mimi says, "Amen brother."

It goes easier after that.
Dad goes through the ceremony.
"Do you Tom take Tom here to be your husband?"
Tom A. nods his head, silent-movie sincere.
"What about you Tom?"
"Yes, I do." He kind of knows this is a joke, doesn't he?
Tom B's pretty smart. He knows that life is filled with
little jokes you have to take serious so that something
means something.
"Well, okay then."
My dad's face is plush and full of pride. I can see all
those people coming at him, then at me. That big airport
hangar or whatever, the red light. In my version, they are
all smiling the way Tom A. does during a blow-job session.
The light is blossoming from all of that, that red light is
blood-light. Love-light. Lava-lamp light. Archie has a
lava lamp in his bedroom, or used to. He would turn it
on in the dark while we made love. "Real cheesy," he
would say. "Just call me your lava-lamp porn stud." The
ceiling would get translucent blisters, like jellyfish were
splattering into themselves.
When they kiss, Tom and Tom in my dad's living room,
it's embarrassing, sure. They kiss long and hard, two
retarded guys kissing really wet. Dad just has to look away.
"That is so sweet," Mimi says.
Salsa says, "Look at those two go at it."
Raquel gets up, goes over and whispers to the two Toms,

and they stop, both out of breath, standing back.

"I now pronounce them Tom and Tom," Dad says.

Raquel comes over.

"I called Motel 6. They have adjoining rooms. I was gonna take them over and stay in the next rom," Raquel says. "But Mimi wants me to go with her. She's in some drag show. You think you could stay with them till I get done?"

Mimi's right next to her, begging me in high style, both long-nailed hands pressed together.

"Sure," I say.

Raquel comes over to me then and hugs me tight, "We are so silly," she whispers. "Ain't we?"

I look at her as we pull apart. She's in her forties but looks about 60. She's about to go bald, her hair is dyed. Those eyes though. I see us at some bar next week laughing about all this.

"We are," I say.

Mimi and Salsa and Raquel go. Dad comes over, holding his head. "Migraine," he whispers. "Tell both Toms goodbye for me. I can't. I'm gonna go to bed."

"Night," I say.

I don't know what else to do but tell them to get into the car. I drive them over to the Motel 6.

Tom B. looks at me in the mirror as I drive.

"We didn't have rings, Anita," he says, like he's just realizing it.

"You know, you're right. We'll have to get you rings

tomorrow. We can go over to K-Mart and get rings." I try to smile.

They start kissing deep again in the backseat.

As soon as I pull into the Motel 6 lot, I tell them to break it up. I check us in. Our rooms are ready. It's doomed, I know, Tom and Tom. Or maybe Tom B. will escape and go and rescue Tom A. from the other group-home. Maybe they'll walk across America and find themselves in paradise.

Tonight's paradise, isn't it? Motel 6's rooms are beige with orange bedspreads. Yellow carpet. They march into their room, and Tom A. in his leisure suit, sits down and grins. Tom B. closes the door to the adjoining room, smiling.

I sit down on my bed and right then is when I see him, standing in the window. Out on the patio.

He starts tapping on the glass.

I can't help it. If he had a crack-pipe I would let him stick it into my mouth, but instead I just let him into the room. He's shivering, he's jailhouse thin. He is in a long cowboy coat and jeans and a cowboy shirt. His eyes look hurt and happy and they seem to glow. My heart feels like all those shaved-headed freaks are marching over it. Love has to happen at the end of every night, or you don't know yourself.

"I'm working," Archie tells me, standing in front of the TV.

I nod my head. "You are huh?"

"Who the hell are they anyway?" Archie asks, and he

comes over and sits down on the bed next to me. "Are they those retarded people you work with? Why'd you bring them here?"

"I just did," I say. "For the hell of it."

Archie laughs. It's wheezy and warm. I want to crawl into his laugh like an orphaned baby onto a luxury liner. Go across the ocean to Europe where some kind lady wants me.

"I love you so much," Archie says. "I should have told you and you could have helped me get off the stuff, but I was just ashamed. I'm sorry for what I did. I lied so much. I was sick, babe. It was like the drug took over, you know?"

I want to tell him to shut up. Want to kick his ass out. That's the next instinct, right after being overjoyed at seeing him, happy at being stalked. I remember when I first met him. It was at a bar in Hamilton, skanky red-neck place me and a girlfriend used to go to shoot darts and get drunk. He was standing by the dart board drinking and smoking, still in his work-clothes, and I threw a dart and it almost got him. But he wasn't pissed.

"Cupid's arrow," he said.

Then Archie and me hear them. Screaming. Silly crazy sex music. There's bumps and thumps against the thin walls. There's laughter.

"Good God," says Archie.

But he isn't disgusted. He isn't even perturbed. He doesn't understand, but he's here with me, and that's next door.

"Are they having a good time or what?" he asks.   He smells of cigarettes and beer and Brut and old pizza and sweat and love.

I guess I love him. I kiss him. That's all I can do.

Lex

I met Lex at the trash dumpster in my trailer park. He said he was a visitor here. I was dumping my garbage, and he went through what I just dumped, with tattered latex gloves on his hands. At first, I wondered if I should call the police.

He had a shaved head, tall, with a black goatee that looked dyed into his skin. His smile was delicate though, and he was wearing a dark blue uniform, possibly from past stints as a night-watchman or janitor.

"Why did you throw this away?" Lex asked, holding up a half-empty bottle of Aqua Velva aftershave. It was shiny green.

"Irritates my skin," I said.

"Do you have running water?" he asked me, pocketing the bottle of aftershave, then taking off his gloves with his teeth.

"Yes I do."

"May I take a shower in your trailer, kind sir?" He laughed, like he really loved playing with words. He scratched at his goatee.

I was an old man. 68. A widower. I looked at him standing in the last of the August sunset, uniformed and shaved-headed. Lex's eyes were what made me go ahead and invite him back to my place. And the smile. Also his arms, which were muscular, a little out of proportion, like Popeye's. There had been a few of these types in my life. Nameless in different places along the way. Before my eyes started going, I drove a semi. Upper-arms thick

as slabs of meat hanging in a butcher-shop, and the faces
in rest areas or far-off state parks, faces as anonymous as
what's left in your dreams when you wake up and go back
to your actual life with a wife and two kids, a boy and a
girl.

"My name is Lex," he said that evening, squinting those
eyes.

We shook hands. He gripped my hand tight. He
possibly knew what I was right then. Maybe loneliness
does something to your skin, or to your grip.

Without saying another thing, Lex followed me on back
to my trailer. It was near the front, and I don't know if
anyone saw us. I kept looking around. Lex's feet made
no sound on the gravel lot, like he was used to sneaking
around. My trailer was newer, a double-wide which I
was thinking about giving to my granddaughter and her
fiancee if they wanted it. I was going to move into one of
those assisted-living places soon.

Lex stepped into my trailer and walked around. The
walls were dark with fake wood paneling. My big
lounger sat real close to my big-screen TV. I still had the
couch from the basement of our old house.

"Turn on the TV," Lex whispered.

I did so.

I sat down, and Lex undid his uniform shirt and
revealed a chest that was smooth and white. He took the
glass bottle of aftershave from his pocket, looked at it like
it was a big green jewel. The light in the room was that
of a closed freezer with one bulb shining. On TV was a

news program about wasteful government spending.

Lex took off his pants. He wore olive-colored boxer shorts, and I felt my mouth fill with spit, and my heart began to squirm as if just shot up with a chemical that does that. I took pills. Lex stood in the middle of the room, looking right at me.

"My dad used to wear this," he said, unscrewing the top of the aftershave bottle with his mouth. He took a deep whiff, and his face went so serious it made my heart stop squirming, although little sparks of pain were still shooting. I stared at Lex's chest and swallowed. Even with my blurry eyesight, I could see what I wanted, and in fact the blur was a nice way to get through being here with him.

"What's your name, sir?" Lex asked, screwing the aftershave's lid back on.

"Roy," I said.

"That was my dad's name, believe it or not," Lex continued whispering in a wise, kind way. "Do you have sugar diabetes, Roy?"

"I don't know," I said, still taking him in. "I had open heart surgery ten months back though."

"Open heart surgery," said Lex, and he came over to me, got into my face. He was sad and sympathetic in a quiet way. Up close, the blur got more defined, and I could make out the thick darkness of his eyebrows, the tunnels that were his nostrils. He was big as a planet right then. My hands shook on the arms of the chair. I froze up, trapped. My heart started feeling worse.

"Roy," Lex said. He kissed my forehead, then leaned away from me, arcing his chest and stomach forward as if he were about to do a backward cartwheel. Then he snapped back into standing straight.

"Shower this way?" He pointed back behind him.

"Yes," I said.

Soon as I heard the water go on, I walked back there. The door was half open, and he said, "Well come on in, Roy."

I sat down on the commode. He pulled the shower curtain back, the water still running. Despite everything, I got a little worried about water dripping onto the floor. But then I allowed myself to take all of him in.

Soap dripped off his shoulders. He was holding his thing in his left hand like it was a hose he was trying to get to come on. He was squeezing it, white lather sliding down his chest and in through the hair down there. Lex did not say one word, however, which I appreciated. I felt my own feeling come out of boxes inside me. Sparkly ghosts spun up out of my stomach, getting heavy up through my heart and esophagus. I felt electrocuted inside. I was very hard down there, and I unzipped carefully. I started in on myself, staring at Lex.

For a second or two, I felt myself dying right there on the commode, dying in a different way. Dying and coming back with the steam of a shower, the smell of an anonymous man using my soap. My heart sped up past itself. I gripped my own thing like it was a rope I would never let go of.

Lex opened his eyes, "You like me, Roy?" He kept squeezing his thing. "You like me?"

"Yeah," I said, jerking at myself.

"You like me, Roy?" Lex started to chant.

I didn't know if I would ever finish. The steam got thicker. Lex was doing it faster and faster to himself. Then his face shook until it was not a face but a kind of glow. He stopped, the stuff shooting out of his thing. My heart reached up into my throat, pounding up into my brain. Finally, I shot out what I had. It wasn't that much, but the power of it coming out reached into my arms through my fingers.

"Roy likes me," Lex whispered.

I kind of crawled away and got into my bed. I was so tired. I heard the water cut off. I heard him in there looking for shaving stuff. It was dark, the sun finally had set, and the trailer park had those nighttime noises of cars scraping over speed-bumps, kids laughing, about to do something mean.

My eyes were so heavy, and my body had knotted up and then unknotted, twisting out of itself. At this point, I couldn't really breath too good.

Before Lex came into the bedroom, I smelled him. He had doused himself in Aqua Velva, that menthol vapor filling up the room. A green smell, like medicine. I think my breathing stopped altogether right then.

"Roy?" he asked me. I looked up at him. He was staring down at me. He had shaved his face clean and smooth. Without the goatee, he looked like a little kid

with something important to do. "Roy, I like you a lot."
I nodded.
"You ready?" he asked me.
I wanted to say, Ready for what? But then I knew.
His mouth opened wide as a door. I knew. There was
something beautiful in being this close to that, in my own
bed. It was a kind of kiss, a kiss for a man with nothing
left to kiss. Nothing at all.

The One I Remember

When he first came here, I thought, this one's a doosey. We all did. We joked about him before he arrived, but that was what we did about all the new ones. Ricky was his name. He was nine years old, and his mom couldn't do it no more. She'd tried to go against what the doctor said, but finally Ricky had busted through a window at her house, 29 stitches. After he was healed up a little, he came to us.

Now this was 1964, so I can tell you right off that we had a buildingful. I was full-time direct-care back then, Building C, that one that had burnt-orange daisies on the walls down the hallways to the bedrooms and the stairs. Of course, at that time, Pinebluff was its own little city, just outside of Wheeling, and I spent much of my life there, I wasn't married, and living with Daddy was like living sometimes with a big baby and other times with a drunk alligator and even other times a pussy-cat-type. But always, always, the man could get on your nerves, even when he was trying to be sweet to you. I buried him eleven years ago. My mom died when I was a girl, maybe cancer, maybe not, nobody told me. I still got the house.

Ricky's mom brought him to us in a big Chevrolet. You'd think that these things don't happen like this, that he would be brought in an ambulance all tied up because he was so crazy, but no she just brought him in with her own mom with her. Her mom was a heavy smoker, and all the way through admitting him she smoked it up. She had on an old blue dress that sagged all over, a

black patent leather purse bigger than her almost, like if
she wanted to she could just fit herself into that purse
and snap it shut and be done with it. Now Ricky he
was okay right then. A little Frankenstein was going on
with part of his face from the window accident, but it
was almost healed like I said, and Ricky was skinny and
healthy otherwise, with a bowl-chopped head of dark hair
and skin the color of Ivory soap. He had those eyes a lot
of them have, almost crossed but not, and of course he was
humming. People with what he had sometimes like to
hum a lot. That's the norm.

His mom was a different case altogether. She sat on the
other side of the social-worker's desk, the social worker
this woman I forget her name. Red-haired and fat and
bossy, and when she died in the tornado five years later
I made a joke in a staff meeting about the wicked witch
and nobody laughed because they were being hypocrites.
Ricky's mom, though, looked like Laura Petrie, you know,
from Dick Van Dyke. Like Mary Tyler Moore before she
found out she was diabetic. I'm not kidding. She was
a class-act, in a black fitted dress, her hair all Jackie-O'd,
and I remember thinking about how this lady didn't look
like she could produce such a child, too class an act, but
then I looked, as I was sent for to keep Ricky in line
during the admission, I looked at Ricky and I saw a lot
of his mother in him. He was quiet, at least now he was,
probably a doctor gave him a shot prior to coming, and
plus that shiny dark hair, and that nice skin. It made me
embarrassed for my own acne skin and how bad a woman

like me would look in a dress like that. It made me
embarrassed like I could hear what my dad was already
saying, That's the truth. But like I said he's been dead
eleven years, but it don't make a difference. Once it's been
said it keeps coming back.

The social worker went through the motions and gave
off that condescending smile people who don't wipe butts
in these places give like: *We are here to help your son learn
to be a normal functioning human-being, Mrs. Campbell.* (This
was Ricky and the lady's last name.) Right. No, that
wasn't it, and we all knew it. We are here, at Pinebluff, to
take your son away because the doctor told you to do this
and there ain't no other way. Because you Mrs. Campbell
can't take it no more. And that's sad, but true.

So I'm holding Ricky's hand through the thing, his dry
almost cold hand, and Mrs. Campbell is signing him in,
and the old lady with them is smoking and holding his
bag of personals on one side, the purse on the other. Mrs.
Campbell finishes and looks up at me.

"Where will he sleep? I mean they showed me when I
came here before but I want to see exactly."

I smile. "We can show you that. Real easy."

I was being nice. I try to be nice as much as possible
but mostly I try to keep my mouth shut. A lady with a
big mouth is—well, you fill in the blank. But let's admit
I do got a big mouth, but with this situation I chose to
be reserved. I had been through what seemed like fifteen
million of these admissions, and the best thing to do is just
keep your trap shut and be like a maid. Be like somebody

they can trust.

The social-worker lady says goodbye after the last piece of paper thank God. She's got some other pressing issues, I guess, so I was told to take them for their tour and to get Ricky settled. Still holding onto my hand, he came right along with me, and Mrs. Campbell and her old decrepit mother followed me through the front offices, which back then were painted the ugliest color of green I think I have ever in my life been exposed to. And there was all that space-age furniture, remember that? Chairs that looked like Russian spacecraft and little dinky tables with black legs and fake-wood-grain tops, low to the ground. Ash-trays all over, thank God, for the old lady, who seemed to be smoking as a way to escape the fact that she was real old and having to go through this.

Then we were going through the offices and outside. It was a sunny cold day in March and the ground was muddy. We had some old trees and some cracked sidewalks and someone the year before had painted a clown mural on a big shed, a clown with balloons. Me and Ricky and Mrs. Campbell and her mom were a little parade going past the church and the school where the kids went, the ones that could get out of bed, past the cafeteria and the nurses' station, and where the office for the doctor was. The buildings back then did not look as they do now. They are pulling people out right and left, and now it's just a damn ghost-town, all boarded up for the most part, and the black paint looks like an X-ray and the rust has eaten through, but right then, in 1964,

Pinebluff was like a little town (I think I said that already). It was like a little town that nobody would want to move into but at least the people in it were still alive. Maybe this made Mrs. Campbell feel better. Probably not.

Ricky was doing okay until we went past the swing-sets. Now they had taken off the swings for winter, but he let go of my hand and run over to them and just let out the highest pitched screaming. His screaming went on and on, even with Mrs. Campbell running over and trying to talk to him in a sweet motherly voice she had. He grabbed hold of one of them chains. And he took that chain hanging down from the pole and he started beating on his head with it and then he jumped up and down, up and down, screaming.

Obviously the shot the doctor gave him wasn't that good, and I just stood back because I had no idea what else to do. In my head I started blaming the social-worker for letting me take them alone. His mom bent down to him and held onto him tight and finally he just quit. The lady's mom held onto her purse and the little sack of personals, and stood right beside her, like she was helping her through childbirth again. The old lady was whispering, "That's it, that's right, you hold onto him. Yes. It's almost over. It's almost over."

Everybody's feet were just covered in mud, by the way. I looked at the feet of everyone, including my own big flat ones, as this was one of those embarrassing moments when you don't know what to say. Finally we start walking again, past the playground, past the greenhouse that we had for the ones that were adults to work in. Now we got a little workshop back here, but they're closing that down too. Out of 200 residents we got 12 left, and they're the really bad ones, the ones who can't talk or walk or eat by themselves. Almost all my Building C people have disappeared, and mainly I work part-time now that I got retirement. I even sometimes think about maybe adopting one of the real bad ones, but I'm just blowing smoke. Me and Pinebluff somehow became the same thing a long while ago. Maybe they ought to bury me here, instead of next to Daddy and Mom.

But back to what I was saying before: now there was the greenhouse, and then Building A and B, and then C. My building. (The other residential buildings went on to D and E, F and G). Let me tell you a little bit about my job at that time. I was head of direct-care for building C but that didn't mean I was anybody's boss. I was just put in charge of getting grunt-work done, and I did it, whether it meant working 80 hours a week or no. Because I was dedicated. Now I know that sounds like I'm patting myself on the back — and go ahead and think that if you want to — but this was my life. Building C, and whether or not that makes me a fruitcake I guess Jesus Christ or whoever on high will judge. But I had my own set of keys. I wore them on my belt loop. Daddy said the keys made me look less ladylike. Not to mention the pants, he said, and that hair. I told him that I might be a bit overweight, and having my hair cut short just made it easier, but I was still ladylike, and if the keys weren't necessary to do my job well then he could have had the gee-dee keys and see if he could pawn them for some booze. That shut him up. Of course later I made him dinner and we watched TV together.

Anyways, there me and Ricky and his mom and her mom are, walking down the hallways of burnt-orange flowers. Down that hall and into the main room, the playroom, where there was a shiny gymnasium floor.

"Now this is where the children have recreation," I said, in my best professional maid's voice. I must have sounded dumb as a box of rocks, but I was willing to take that risk.

"Nice," the old woman said, lighting up again.

Mrs. Campbell looked terrified. She was holding Ricky's hand now. Ricky was jerking it a little, like he knew what was about to happen.

"And we have a swimming pool in Building D. Inside. It's heated too. Does Ricky like to swim?"

"No," Mrs. Campbell said, looking around.

"He can learn," the old lady said, smiling for the first time.

I went on with them past the three bedrooms on the ground floor up to the second. Now the residential buildings were two-stories and had three bedrooms on the bottom and four on top, with the girls in the three downstairs, the boys upstairs. Ricky would be sharing a room with three other boys; for the total in Building C there was 16 boys and 9 girls. The arrangements worked out pretty good. Today the kids were all in their bedrooms, except for a few that had been taken outside by the field to get air, so when we had walked past the girls' rooms we saw a couple cuties, Tricia and Monique, both Down's girls, sitting in their room rocking and one of them holding crayons. Sally and Helen and Darla and Kate were all in bed. Now upstairs the boys were in their rooms. There was, let's see, Mikey and Andy and Sam, and I remember Tom and Lincoln and J.D. But that's outside of the realm of what I'm telling you still, and I'm trying my best to stay on track, so I'll skip remembering all their names, although we have Lincoln and Sam with us still.

Finally the four of us were in Ricky's bedroom, the one he'd be staying in. He shared a room with Tom and Peter and the other one I think was Darrel, yeah Darrel. All three of them died back in the early seventies. They were all three mostly in bed most of the time because one had cerebral palsy and the spina-bifida, which made his spine grow outside his body, and the other was born missing the part of his brain that let him walk and talk. That was Peter. He had eyes and nose and all that, and he had a sweet way of moving his mouth. But he could not speak and spit foamed out of his mouth all the time, but he was lovable.

Mrs. Campbell gripped Ricky's hand so tight I bet it hurt. But Ricky seemed to like that.

The grandmother was saying, "These rooms are big."

"Yes," I said.

The grandmother, cigarette ash dangling off the cigarette in her mouth (I wanted to tell her to put that thing out but it was too touchy a situation so I let it go), put Ricky's things on his twin hospital bed. We were all quiet as the night before Christmas. I don't know, like I said prior, I had been through hundreds of these type of things and yet this time I felt I could not look. Maybe it was her Mary Tyler Moore looks. Or the old lady pushing on her to keep going. But I felt like this was the sad one, the one I would remember. Well I was right.

Ricky started humming louder. Ricky started humming, I'll always remember his humming. I will.

Then this was when Ricky got onto the bed after taking his hand away from his mom. I remember this part pretty damn good too. I thought his mom was going to try to stop him but she didn't. He climbed up on the bed and he just started going after it and I mean he jumped up and he jumped down and he would not stop. I thought of a rhyme we had in grammar school: *Two little monkeys were jumping on the bed / One fell off and busted his head / Momma called the doctor and the doctor said / That's what you get for jumping on the bed*. I heard little taunting kid voices singing that. I think at that moment I was in a state of heart-sickness, watching him and hearing those voices. But these things always pass, I thought at the time.

His mom stood beside the bed and she was looking at him and she was starting to sob. The grandmother was saying, "Tell him to stop it, Martha. Don't let him act like that."

But Mrs. Campbell was not crying really. She was crying, sure, she'd probably been crying all day, but she was also laughing. The mix made her look crazy. Because there was joy in her face when he jumped up and down on the bed. This joy I think caught her by accident, in the middle of all this. The kid was laughing, best he could do laughing-wise. He was grunting and he was screaming. I looked around at the others in their beds, the ones who didn't get out of bed much but to be turned so they wouldn't get no bed-sores, and I felt sorry for them more than usual. I mean it was like I didn't really know these people but I loved them and I realized that with a big blast to my head, and I wanted them to be able to jump like that. Jump like that and out of here. Jump up through the god-dern ceiling and disappear.

There was like these few seconds or so of suspended — what is that astronauts get into? — suspended animation? That's what it was like.

Finally I had to get involved before my other staff came in and saw this.

I said, "He might fall, Mrs. Campbell."

Mrs. Campbell said, "No he won't."

Her mother said, "He'll fall, Martha. Let this lady take care of it."

So I went over. I stopped him. I grabbed ahold of him. Then at that moment — maybe he thought I was somebody who loved him — he hugged me so tight I was about ready to push him away. I remember he smelled of pee and good clean shampoo.

Mrs. Campbell ran out. The grandmother came over and grabbed hold of Ricky's hand and shook it like a doll's hand.

She said, "We'll visit. We will."

Well there you go. I don't know if this is a story or not, but I got down what I wanted to. I could go into the rest in great detail, as you know already, but I won't. There ain't much to tell, but there's everything too. Ricky had a life with me and the staff at Pinebluff for awhile, but he got wilder and wilder and finally they started doing the shock therapy to him and he got shipped off to somewheres else. That was 1967. I don't really remember the exact day he left by any means, because I think sometimes your brain stops you from remembering things that can make you go crazy. I don't want to tell you anymore about his crazy episodes either because first it probably is none of your business and second I want you to remember him on this one other day when Mrs. Campbell came to visit him.

I remember her being in a cashmere sweater, and it was fall. We were out at a picnic table. She had brought him jelly donuts. His favorites. I was working that day, thank God. This time her mom didn't come with her. I wondered if Mrs. Campbell had a husband or if maybe her husband had left her after Ricky was born. I wondered if her husband maybe stayed at home too sad, or if her husband right then was with some other lady, with a new baby, a new life, and Mrs. Campbell was here visiting Ricky as her only way to stay sane. This was maybe a year into his stay with us, and at that time he was all right, at least most of the time. So she had on this cashmere sweater and there was the jelly donuts. I remember him with jelly all over his face. I remember her eating one too. Daintily. She was very pretty.

I remember saying, "This is not your fault." Out of the blue, like I even knew her.

She looked up. Ladies like her nibbled, so she was nibbling on her donut. She looked up.

I remember her saying, "Yes it is."

But it wasn't like she was feeling guilty maybe. She just did not want me bullshitting her. And I wanted to thank her for that, as the world mostly is full of bull, is it not? I mean I don't want to sound like I'm complaining, but really when you get down to it it is. I mean the world has its moments, yes, but....

But then he had his jelly donuts and then there was a pile of dead leaves somebody had raked up and I saw her reach over to him and pick him up. She and him, she let this happen, they fell backwards into the leaves. Her and her son, in the leaves from the trees at Pinebluff. Remember that. He was screaming, but so was she. They both were.

Where You Live

The first time I saw Tim conscious, he was listening to music on a Walkman, in a wheelchair in a mint-green waiting room. His long, black hair was unwashed and uncombed, and the hospital gown came up over his bony knees. I walked up to him.

"Yeah?" he said, pulling the head-phones off.

"The nurse said you were here."

Tim nodded. "I'm here. I'm still here. What, you an ambulance guy?"

I was in the regulation orange overalls. "Yes. I was the one, I mean, this other guy, my partner and I, we were the ones who got your call."

Tim turned off the music.

"I'm Gene Hampton," I said.

"Tim.... What? I'm supposed to say, thank you so very much, right?" He smiled, then flipped the tape over.

I sat down on a vinyl chair facing him. We were quiet. The music blasted on.

After a few minutes, Tim flicked the tape off again and looked into my eyes. "You're wondering why I did it. It's like, you're thinking, I guess he was really depressed about his grades at school. Or maybe it's because he's without a loving family atmosphere to support him."

I didn't say anything.

Tim stared at me, his eyes widening. "You have a crush on me, don't you?" he said. "You're a goddamned faggot." Tim smiled angrily. "You are, aren't you?"

I didn't move.

A month and a half later, Tim was in the kitchen of a halfway-house, shuffling a deck of Uno cards at a long picnic table, dressed in a Nine Inch Nails t-shirt and a pair of ragged sweat-pants. Tim's dark hair was shaved to the scalp now. He looked up as I cleared my throat.

"Eugene," he said, faking surprise.

I smiled.

"It's Eugene, everybody!" Tim laughed loudly.

I turned to see if anybody were listening. A social-worker named Don lived here, skinny in long sweaters and khaki pants usually carrying a clipboard, but he wasn't around. Most of the other guys were sitting in the blurry living room, inhaling each other's second-hand smoke, watching JAG.

"I just came to see you, okay?"

Tim stood up, the kitchen chair squawking. He snapped a rubber-band around the Uno cards. "Let's go somewhere."

In a brown booth at the back of a Denny's, Tim poured a creamer into his third cup of coffee, his hands shaky.

"What do you do with the rest of your life?" he said. "I mean, when you aren't getting into my pants?"

"I work seventy hours a week. I've told you that," I said.

"Yeah, but how do you fucking see me all the time?"

"I see you when I should be sleeping."

"Where do you live anyway?" Tim eyed me intensely; then his stare landed on the edge of the table.

"Nowhere. Out in the country," I said.

Tim laughed. "What in a barn?"

"Close. With my mom and dad. Off the interstate. They used to run the farm, but now they rent out the land to other people. I've lived there all my life."

"Twenty-three and still live at home. Does that qualify you as a total loser?" Tim lit a cigarette, then dragged off of it, and a few seconds later smashed it out.

"I guess," I said.

"Poor baby," Tim said, shoving the rest of his fish sandwich into his mouth.

I gazed down at my used silverware. I wanted to leave suddenly, but then I pictured Tim, the first time I saw him, in the basement of the house his foster-parents owned. Tim had swallowed twenty-six sleeping pills he'd stolen from his foster-mom, and stripped down to his underwear, lying on the concrete floor near the water-heater. The lights were out, and his pale body glowed in the blue gas flame.

Tim was standing now, putting on his natty sweater.

"Let's get out of here," he said, walking away from the table, his shoulders slightly stooped. He never doubted that I would follow him.

In the car, Tim was silent.

"Where do you want to go?" I asked. We were on the interstate, and the darkness glittered with passing semi lights.

"I really don't care." He belched, then shoved a tape out of his pocket into my tape-player. Thrashing music spilled out of the tapedeck, and Tim turned it up, looking out the other window.

I found myself driving near where I lived.

"Where are we?" Tim asked, turning the stereo down. "Bumfuck, Egypt?"

I laughed, thinking of my mom and dad the Sunday afternoons when they came home from church. My mom's eyes were always worried, my dad not looking at me. Me in pajamas and a robe eating pot-roast, little potatoes and carrots in a solemn kitchen.

"Where the fuck are we going?" Tim said.

"Just driving," I said.

Tim laughed. "This is where you live, isn't it?"

I didn't answer. Big maple trees, naked in winter, snow-covered turned over soil, aluminum-sided houses passing. Tim turned off the music.

"All this time, you tried to keep it a secret," Tim said.

"Keep what a secret?" I turned on my brights.

"Who you really are. I mean, you know me. You know I'm a suicidal teenaged orphan boy with a child-abuse past living at this time in a halfway house in Muncie, Indiana. But now, I get to see you for real. It's like Batman taking me to the Batcave, right?"

I pulled over at the side of the road before reaching my house. We were near a ditch. Shivering, I did not understand exactly what I was doing. Tim got out first and started beating his chest like Tarzan.

"Shut up," I said.

The road was slushy. We leaned against the car-hood, looking up at the sky, our breath steaming. Then Tim

took off into the woods, and I followed him. I kept
flashing back even though I didn't know what I was
flashing back to, until finally after walking through the
muddy paths with vines and creepers slapping into our
faces we reached an abandoned graveyard. I remembered
a boy named Scott, when Scott and I were both fourteen,
and it was summer, and we would jerk off back here in
the privacy of crooked tombstones and shady trees. Now
the winter made all of it seem deader, the naked trees
bending in with the weight of icicles.

"Cool," Tim said.

I stood by a tombstone the shape of a tower, with
someone's name engraved in it, the years of birth and
death. Tim kicked at one of the stones, and it flopped
over. Yelling Karate sounds, Tim kicked several more
stones. Then he stopped. He walked over to me and laid
down in front of the tombstone I was standing beside, put
his hands on his chest in a tranquil gesture. I bent down
to him and kissed him on the mouth deeply, and pulled
at his jeans and then he was naked, mud covering his
backside; I did not want this to happen, but as it happened
I felt the intensity of it like a fever sprouting. I got naked
too. His flesh was warm next to the cold mud. I kissed
the dip in the bones on his left shoulder. We did it like
animals.

Afterwards, Tim was standing beside a tree getting
dressed, hopping as he put a sock on. I got up too and
put on my pants. I couldn't find my other sneaker in the
dark, and Tim lit his cigarette lighter. His face floated in

the nervous yellow of the lighter.

"Here it is," he said. He threw the shoe at me, and it hit my forehead. I bent down and picked it up, and when I stood up, I called his name, but he had disappeared.

"Tim?" I said it over and over, walking through the woods, until finally I was out of them, on the road, almost in front of my parent's house. I saw Tim on my front porch, knocking. I immediately stepped back, hiding behind some trees. My mom came out of the door. I could barely see her face, but could tell she was not smiling. Tim was animated, talking to her. I wondered if he was telling her about me, what we had been doing. I remembered nights when Scott and I would do it in my bedroom, and I would think that my parents could hear through the heat registers, our passionate whispers working their way through the small tunnels in the house.

But then my mother slammed the door. I could hear Tim laughing. He walked off the porch, toward where I had parked the car, and I ran to him.

"What the fuck were you doing?" I asked, as I started the car.

Tim didn't say anything. He pushed the tape back in. I turned it off.

"What in the hell?" I said, but my anger felt fake and weak.

Tim smiled at me. "I saw the name on the mailbox, and I went up there, and I told your mom that I was the angel of death and that I was making a motherfucking housecall." He laughed. "She freaked of course. She said

she would call the police and that she wasn't going to
have any of this. And then I said I had the wrong house,
sorry."

I stared at the road. I felt pity for my mom as we got
back onto the highway. No one could win with Tim. I
could see my mom's face in close-up being frightened
by this kid, a shaved, mud-covered freak coming out of
nowhere.

I loved him, I knew that now more than ever.

At first we watched TV in the Motel 6 room, sitting on
the brown bed. I wanted to take a shower right away, but
Tim kept telling me to fuck off. We were mud-covered
and sweaty, and I thought a hot shower would sedate us. I
kept trying to tell him this, but he said, "Shut up, asshole.
Watch the cartoon." As he watched TV, he quietly bit his
fingernails.

After the cartoon, Tim stood up and shut the TV off.
He took his shirt and pants off. The mud on his body
had dried. I stood up, and he pushed me back down. He
stood there in his loose, gauzy underwear, his face sulky.
He looked decimated, his ribs gleaming through in curves,
the mud like splashy tattoos, his head shaved into that
black-stubble dome.

In the shower, both of us were very quiet. I watched
him soap himself, the white soap turning brown in his
hands. I could love only Tim, I knew, washing his head
with soap, kissing it. He washed me. The water got so
hot that our skin tingled as if on fire.

Mom was still up when I got home. All the lights in the house were on, and Dad was in his work-pants and t-shirt, an outfit he wore still even after retiring. His shotgun was leaning against the La-Z-Boy, and the TV was on too loud on CNN Headline News. Mom was in her housecoat, holding onto her arms.

"The police were here," Mom said.

"What?" I said.

I looked at the clock above the TV. It was 3:56 in the morning.

"I had to call the police," Mom said. "Some boy came over here tonight and he threatened to kill us."

Dad got up. He looked pale, his face jowly. "I'm telling you what, you just can't escape this violence," he said. "You'd think living out here, it wouldn't be a problem. But I'll be damned if it's not got out here now."

Mom went into the kitchen. Dad turned the TV off.

"Your mom can't get to sleep," he said. He pointed to his gun, then said loudly, so Mom could hear, "We're protected. The police said there wasn't anything they could do, but we're protected."

"Yes," I said.

Mom came out with a glass of water. "I tell you," she said. "I need to get to sleep."

I said, "I'm sorry this happened."

Mom sipped her water. "I tell you that boy I just, I mean, he just came out on the porch like it was his house and he says to me, 'I am the angel of death,' laughing. He was crazy. Crazy." Mom laughed nervously, then gulped the rest of her water.

Dad said, "Calm down. It's okay."

Mom looked at me directly in the eye. "I swear to God. I about had a heart-attack. You would had to run out here and resuscitate me." She laughed nervously.

I smiled at her, feeling crazy. A terrible hatred floated up into my mind, like helium, hot and effervescent, blending in with my other feelings, then deadening them. I thought of Tim's practiced-mean smile: the angel of death. The room was stuffy and too bright, and Dad said, again, as if part of a chant none of us could believe, "We're protected."

Before going home, I had dropped Tim off at the halfway house, the sloppy Victorian at the end of a small garbage-strewn street. Before going in, Tim walked over to the driver's side of the car and stuck his head in, kissing me deeply on the mouth.

"You're fucking crazy, Eugene," he whispered.

I didn't say anything.

"That's why I stick with you," he said. "You saved my life and now I'm saving yours. Remember? Goddamn, I was dead and you come and blow into my mouth. You CPR me. Pump my stomach. Brought me back from the valley of death so you could fuck me."

I looked at him for a minute, not knowing what to say. He grinned at me.

"That's right. You are out of your mind. Taking me out there, man. That was perfect. Now I know where you

live and I can come and visit you anytime I want, right?"
He saluted me in front of the car, in the white glare of the
headlights. "You and me," he said. "We love each other."

I watched him walk up the stairs to the house, taking
three or four steps at a time. He pounded on the door of
the huge dark house, yelling, "Open up boys! It's me. I'm
home!"

Spider In the Snow

On our way home from the mall that day before
Christmas Eve, a coyote ran out in front of us from a
field beside the highway. I think I might have made eye
contact for a fraction of a second. After we hit the thing,
Candy, my new live-in girlfriend, pulled the car over, and
we got out and looked for it. But it was nowhere to be
found.

"Poor thing," Candy said when we got back into the
car. She was all emotional.

"You gonna be okay?"

"I'd like to know where it went," she said, dabbing her
eyes with a Kleenex from the glove compartment.

"Off by itself to lick its wounds," I said, trying to sound
like I knew something.

Back at the house, as soon as she got done wrapping my
daughters' Christmas gifts for me (she'd helped me pick
out purses for both at the mall), Candy still seemed shook
up.

"They keep building those new houses out there by
the interstate, and what do they expect? All they're doing
is making the poor things run out into the road to their
deaths. I didn't even know there could be coyotes in
Ohio."

"They get around," I said. I appreciated Candy's outrage
and her sensitivity, don't get me wrong, but I saw the
animal in my mind, spotty-furred and wild with a busted
head, peering into people's living room windows with an
extreme and hungry lonesomeness, and I just wanted to
forget the whole incident. Move on.

"Don't worry about it," I whispered. "Let me take your mind off it. Come on."

I led her into my bedroom she'd just help me redecorate, fancy and floral but also refined. Made her sit on the plush bedspread.

"What are you doing Jerry?" Candy said, half-smiling.

I went into the bathroom and got the hairbrush and hair spray. I gave them to her.

"Do my hair for me for my trip," I said, sitting down on the floor in front of her.

I had really nice hair, Candy was always telling me. She was a licensed beautician, so she ought to know. In fact, we'd met each other at her salon, where I'd gone to have the gray dyed out. Now, the brush going through my thick, naturally curly hair was like the sun chasing a cloud, smooth and silent. Candy worked with delicate and professional motions. Toward the end she had me get up and go into the bathroom so she could shave my neck.

"You really do have the prettiest hair," she said, after the neck-shave. She guided me toward the mirror above the sink, and I had to agree. I could see Candy behind me in the reflection. She took really good care of herself, a walking advertisement for her own skills: skillfully dyed and coiffed blonde hair, perfect mauve nails, make-up done expertly, only the best clothes. I happen to be a short but well-built guy. Candy is quite tall, close to six feet. The height difference had been a big obstacle for her at first.

We went back into the bedroom, to bed, for a little rest

and relaxation. To be off till the morning after Christmas, I'd had to work a double yesterday at Old Country Buffet, the restaurant I manage, so I was a little tired. We both laid back onto the mattress, and I rolled over and kissed her.

"Careful," she whispered. "Don't mess your hair up, hon."

Day before yesterday, I'd called my two daughters up to wish them a long distance Merry Christmas, but then for some reason Regina, my sixteen year old, grabbed the phone from Michelle, my sweet little eleven year old, and said, "Are you coming Daddy? Oh please come!"

Regina's voice is gruff yet sweet. She is a big girl, a bit overweight.

I said, "For Christmas?"

"Yes dummy."

"Are you coming or not?" Irene, my ex, was on the other extension, listening in.

"Well, I wasn't really planning on it."

"You never see them, Jerry," Irene said.

I heard Regina grunt on the phone she was using, "Do not antagonize him Mom."

Regina was always running away, like many teenaged daughters of divorce.   Irene continually reported it to me when it happened usually with messages on my machine like: "Regina's gone again. Run off with that girl. Just thought you'd like to know." Click.

I ended up saying, "I hadn't planned on coming, but I

guess I could."

Irene said, "I put up a real tree this year. Decorated
the inside and the outside of the house. I'm in between
boyfriends, so I got a lot of time on my hands." She
laughed, and I could hear her lighting up a cigarette.
"How's your new girlfriend? I mean, it is a girl, isn't it?"

"Candy. Her name is Candy," I said, but I put that
dead-end tone into it. We were definitely not going there.

Michelle took hold of the phone then and screamed,
"We'll make lasagna!"

That was my specialty. I got a little choked up from her
remembering.

Although she was still a bit shaken from the coyote
incident, Candy drove me to the station to give me a
nice bon-voyage. The only bus I could catch going to
Tennessee out of Cincinnati was at ten o'clock, and
around eight that night it started to snow. The downtown
depot was dismal on the inside, half-demolished on the
north side, from some unfinished remodeling. Concrete
and steel beams were exposed and everything over on that
side seemed dusty and bombed-out.

When we got to my gate (after checking my one
suitcase in), I stepped up to Candy while she was tying
her plastic scarf back under her chin. I held onto the girl's
wrapped gifts, which we'd put into a big plastic grocery
bag. She smelled of raspberry hair spray and Juicy Fruit
gum and White Diamonds. I was gonna miss this lady.
She was going to her brother's tomorrow for Christmas

in Middletown, so I knew she would not be alone, but
still my heart felt a peculiar ache. I guess it was about
how I never really wanted to be responsible for anybody's
loneliness.

I got on tip-toes to kiss her, enjoying the stretch in my
calf muscles.

"Have a good Christmas with your girls," Candy
whispered, pulling back. "When you get back, I'm gonna
have a special Christmas present for you."

"What?" We were going to celebrate our Christmas
when I got back the day after.

"Never mind. Just wait."

Walking backwards and blowing me a kiss, Candy
bumped into a tall, slouchy guy with a shaved head in
a pair of black jeans and combat boots and a long black
trench-coat, standing by an out-of-order pop machine.
Candy winked and apologized and walked on. The guy
looked over towards me and winked.

"Pretty lady," he said.

"Yup," I said.

About fifteen minutes after she left, there was an
announcement that my bus was not gonna be showing up
till around midnight, if that. They had had to shut down
a part of the interstate in Kentucky due to running out of
road salt.

"Snow," a low-pitched voice whispered close behind
me.

I was at the back window, staring out at the huge
cascading flakes after calling Irene to let her know about

the delay. I turned around, and the guy in the combat boots and trench-coat was standing right there.

I laughed, "Doesn't this just plain suck?"

The guy's face was pale, his eyes shiny and deep-set and crystal blue, a cleft in his chin like Kirk Douglas. He had pulled the trench-coat halfway-off to reveal a faded Spiderman t-shirt, his gut hanging out from the bottom of it.

"You smoke?" he said.

"Yeah, but I ran out." (I was lying. I had recently quit at the request of Candy.)

"You can bum one."

We walked out to the front, where a couple other guys were smoking. Big, cold sparks of snow blew into my face. He lit my cigarette for me. I took a big drag, holding onto my garbage bag of gifts.

"I'm Kent," he said.

"Jerry," I said.

We smoked together out there in the snow, and I found out we were both on the same bus, and he was going to see an old Army friend for Christmas. I told him a little bit about my daughters. Then Kent flung his half-smoked cigarette out into the curtain of snow.

"Fuck, it's cold. I wish you could smoke in-doors." There was a sad plea for mercy in his voice. "Come on," he said.

I knew what would happen next. I always did know in situations such as this. We walked into the bathroom together. I did what he did with his bag of clothes: put my bag of gifts up on a stainless steel shelf at the front of the bathroom.

After two faceless men left, Kent opened the stall door, went in. I followed, the hand-blower still going. I was shaking a little.

"No better way to pass the time," he whispered, enclosed in gray-green written-on metal walls. "My nickname is Spider," he whispered. "Welcome to my web."

"Spider?"

"I'm into Spiderman," he said, pointing at his shirt, like I was an idiot. Then he took his shirt off. His belly looked pregnant, but I did not care.

Someone came in. We froze. I knew whoever came in could see four feet under the stall pretty easy, but knowing this did not prevent me from moving toward him very slowly, as if the closer we got, our four feet would merge into two. I smelled his skin, a hint of smoke and onion.

After Spider and I did our business, we went to the shelf at the front. Spider's bag of clothes was still there, but the gifts were gone.

"Oh God," I said. "Oh dear God."

"What?"

"My stuff's gone."

"That sucks," Spider said.

I shook Spider awake when they finally called for passengers. It was almost four AM.

"Goddam," he said. "What?" His expression, right from

bus-station sleep, was grouchy and baby-like.

"The bus is here." I smiled.

I walked on out to the bus and stepped into its interior, right behind an Amish lady and her two sons who took seats up front. I sat down midway through, moving toward the window so Spider could sit down, but Spider passed by me, going to the back. We took off after a couple minutes. I turned my head toward the back but could not see him. I kept thinking of the girl's gifts, how I should have gone to the police or told somebody in charge, but then again I'd known that if they found the guy who took the gifts — wouldn't he tell on Spider and me? Wouldn't I be totally humiliated?

Finally I fell to sleep, woke up to blurry, white light coming in through all the windows, the smell of winter-coated bodies and sleep. Snow was still falling, but the road was mostly clear. We weren't on an interstate, just a smaller highway in Kentucky. A few minutes later, the bus came to a stop near a backwoods gas station that did not seem to be open. The driver's voice over the PA system came on: "This is not a rest stop, folks. Just a passenger drop off."

People sat back down. Spider stayed up. The snow fell a little thicker here, blurring the view of the closed down gas station with cigarette posters in the windows. Spider walked past me without saying anything. Jumped out.

I strained my neck to see through the windows on the other side.

There he was, walking in the snow, holding his paper

sack of clothes, his head bent away from the bus. I wondered when his old Army buddy would be picking him up. Then I wondered who he even was. And who I was. What we had done back there. I saw him stripped naked and pale in that stall, flabby belly and skinny arms, his eyes closed tightly as he did the most intimate thing you can do with another human being, the closed-off smile right when it was over, and he started slipping back into his own skin and his underwear, saying under his breath, "Wow. Wow. That was great. Thanks. Yeah. I needed that."

"Me too," I had said.

"Daddy!" Regina yelled. She and a lanky girl in sweats with long hair braided back were waiting outside the bus station for me in Johnson City, Tennessee.

I was shocked seeing Regina, ready to go over to the drugstore to buy her and her sister's replacement presents before they picked me up, but then there she and that girl were, waiting in front of a rust-bucket Escort parked beside the curb. It was warm here. Snow was melting away already, the sun shining. Regina came running toward me. She had gained a lot of weight since I'd last seen her. She was now not just fat but morbidly obese, as they say.

The girl behind her was looking down at the ground. Regina hugged me and kissed me.

"Daddy!" She was laughing with the utmost joy. I felt small and insignificant, but with really good hair I'd tried to keep nice even riding on a bus.

"Hey baby," I said.

A big smile was locked onto her face. The girl with her was solemn and quiet.

"Where's Michelle?" I said. I held onto my suitcase.

"Home. This is Amber," Regina said, pulling Amber closer to meet me.

"Hey," she said.

Regina pulled our hands together so we could shake. Amber kept her eyes always pointed at the ground.

"Mom said she was gonna pick you up, but I told her I would. I wanted to talk to you before Mom got hold of you," Regina said.

Amber rolled her eyes and whispered, "Bitch."

"I know," Regina said, turning her gaze back to me. "Mom is being a bitch."

"Oh, now," I said.

"Come on, I'll tell you the whole stupid story in the car, Daddy," Regina said.

Even though she was big and heavy, she had an energy about her, probably because she was mad and not getting her way. She had on tight jeans and a sweat shirt with teddy bears on it and her hair was kinked up with a perm. Regina wore lip gloss too, eye shadow, cheap looking stuff compared to what Candy wore. She looked too old to be a girl and yet there was a girlish quality about her that was almost frightening, like she was trying way too hard to be alive.

Amber grabbed my suitcase and carried it for me. I

guess this is something she just wanted to do. I got into the Escort. Amber, after putting my suitcase in the hatchback, got into the driver's seat. The interior smelled of cigarettes really bad, and sure enough as soon as both girls got in they lit up from the same pack. They had big Styrofoam cups of coffee in strategically placed cup holders. Cigarette in her mouth, Regina turned back toward me, her bulk preventing her from placing her chin on the top of bucket seat like she seemed to be wanting to do.

"Mom won't let Amber stay for Christmas with us. She keeps telling her to go, and I'm just like sick of it Daddy. I want you to tell her how much me and Amber love each other. I want this whole Mom stuff to end."

"Well, we'll see."

Regina laughed, "Come on. Daddy. Me and you are gay, and we need to stand up for ourselves, okay?"

"Regina," I said.

"What?"

"I'm bi."

"Whatever," she said. "You know what I mean."

She turned back around and took a big drink from her Super America cup of coffee.

Johnson City passed by the windshield: old small-town courthouse and Winn Dixie and roller-rink and firehouse turning into weeds at the outskirt of the mountains. I remembered coming down here with Irene and the girls for Christmases when they were both little. How this place seemed foreign and special to me with its mountains

and Southern accents and little country stores.   Irene
had moved up to Ohio when she was fourteen with her
parents, but once we split, she decided she wanted to go
back home to her country roots.

The highway went over a hill, then down into the valley
where Darlene, Michelle and Regina lived. She'd told
me they were renting a house now that she had her new
job as a door-to-door phlebotomist. It was beautiful out
here. I was blocking out what Regina had said, the gay
thing, but still I remembered how Irene had told both my
daughters, back three years ago when we separated, that I
was gay. I had stressed with both girls the bisexual issue.
Irene had always known I was bi. But in all actuality the
main reason Irene wanted divorced was that she had
caught me in the bathroom with some old guy at where
I used to work (a pancake house I managed, prior to
moving onto Old Country Buffet). She'd always told me
as long as I kept the bi-thing under control, as in looking
and not touching, she could take it, and even sometimes
we would comment to each other on the cute guys at the
mall.

But that one night Irene came to pick me up due to
my car being in the shop. I'd thought I had locked the
front door. I thought this guy and I could have a little
quickie before Irene showed up. It meant nothing, just
a way to decompress, to forget the everyday stress of
managing a restaurant. This guy was not handsome, but
he was willing, a waiter with salt-and-pepper hair and one
earring.

All the other employees had gone home. We started doing it in the men's room. The battery in my watch was dead, so I did not know how late it was. I guess Irene got tired of waiting outside in the car. She came into the restaurant, eventually wound up knocking on the men's room door. We were trapped. The waiter with the salt-and-pepper hair and I tried a strategy of silence, but Irene finally barged in.

Irene did not say one word. Just backed up out of the men's room, and then outside in the hallway after the door slammed shut, she screamed, "You can walk your ass home, buddy. This little charade called a marriage is over."

The house they were renting was in a little addition near Doe River. Big dead-tree mountain formations, sloppy from melted snow, surrounded the neighborhood. All the houses were the same, except painted different colors, two- or three-bedroom ranch-styles, surrounded by lots of yard and gravel. Irene was not kidding when she said she had decorated. There were lights upon lights strung up on the roof and gutters and bushes, and even though it was morning they were turned on.

Regina took the electric garage door opener out of her purse, pressed the button.

"I hope Dutchess doesn't have another seizure," she said.

Dutchess was our German Shepherd dog. I mean, the dog we used to have together as a family.

"Seizures?" I said.

Amber said, pulling into the garage, "Yeah. Whenever

she hears the garage door open. At least that's what we're thinking."

We all got out, and Regina asked me one more time, "Please Daddy. Talk to her. I am a gay teenager. I could end up killing myself."

Her huge, outraged, and totally sincere face saddened and frightened me. I remembered the feeling I had when the divorce got final and they moved away, how relieved I was, not sad or tore up emotionally, but relieved. Guilty yet relieved. Wondering why and how I had ever become a father in the first place.

"Okay honey. I will."

All three of us walked in, and as soon as we did I heard Irene yell from the basement: "Come down here, you all."

The door to the basement was directly to the right. A baby gate had been taken down, leaning against the kitchen table. The house had a musty smell, but the kitchen itself was sparkling clean. I got a view of the living room down the hall, which, like the outside, was decorated to the max with lights and a tree and all kinds of elaborate touches.

Michelle came running up the basement steps, screaming joyfully. She was small for her age, with blonde, stringy hair and a sweet face. She hugged me tight.

"Daddy," she said. "We're gonna make lasagna tonight aren't we?"

"Yup."

We all walked down the steps together to the paneled walls, green wall-to-wall carpet, a couch with a TV.

Dutchess was lying beside the TV, shivering on the floor, on her back, all four legs twitching in different directions. Irene was standing over Dutchess, in her door-to-door phlebotomist's uniform. She was fatter even than Regina. Her eyes had big bags.

"Look at this," she said.

Dutchess was quiet, except for a low growl that did not seem to be coming from her mouth. I saw poop sliding slowly out of her tail-end. Pee had spread out under her on the carpet. Her eyes were open but completely white. I thought automatically of the coyote yesterday morning, the logic of hitting a wild dog one day, and then a dog I have always known having seizures the next. It was like karma, if you believed in that sort of thing.

"It's definitely the garage door opener, girls," Irene said.

Amber went and got a pillow from the couch to put under Dutchess's head, but Irene said, "That is not necessary. It'll get puke on it."

Amber whispered fuck-you under her breath, putting the pillow back.

"See?" Regina said. "See Daddy? See how Mom treats my girlfriend?"

Irene laughed. "They are gonna try to play us off each other, Jer."

"Looks like it," I said.

Regina game me the evil eye. Dutchess continued through her seizure. Michelle was grabbing onto my side, whispering toward the dog, "Poor baby. Poor thing."

I looked right at Irene and said, "I hope that all of us can

have a good holiday. Amber included." I tried to smile.
Regina applauded.

Irene just grunted and stooped down to Dutchess,
petting her.

"She's been doing this since three weeks back. I took
her to the vet, and he's ordered tests. He said he may have
to put her on pills that will knock her out and ruin the
quality of her life. I swear it's when she hears the garage
door go up, you know, she gets all excited knowing we're
home. And it just overheats her brain. Plus she's old."

Irene stood up real slow and looked over at Regina.
"We all know the real problem I have with Miss Amber."

Amber just laughed defiantly. Regina finally burst into
a big round of tears. Michelle went down to the floor to
be with Dutchess.

"Mom!" Regina yelled.

Irene stepped over toward me and Regina.

"Stop being homophobic!" Regina screamed. "Think
of Matthew Shepard!"

"I'm not homo-whatever-you-want-to-call-it. I'm
not. God knows I'm not. I'm letting your daddy stay
here in this house for Christmas, for God sakes! Your little
girlfriend over there stealing from my gosh-darn purse.
That's my problem. I don't care if you two are gay or
from Mars. I don't. I just cannot stand a thief."

"You're such a liar," Regina said, and then the two of
them, Regina and Amber, took off up the basement steps.

Irene turned to me, smiling, "Merry Christmas." She

laughed, so did I. I mean, what else could you do?

Small-boned and delicate, Michelle was holding Dutchess's head on the floor. The dog seemed to wake up from her trance just because Michelle was holding her. Dutchess's eyes were now shutting and opening, losing their glassy whiteness. She was almost ready to yawn.

Michelle was whispering down to her black, pointy ears, "You're okay. You're okay."

Michelle and I went to the grocery for Christmas Eve lasagna ingredients. Irene let me drive her car, and inside it was scattered with all her blood-taking paraphernalia, red sharps containers and plastic sheathed vials and Xeroxed documentation sheets. Michelle helped me put all this stuff in the trunk.

"Mom's so messy," she said in her little girl way.

I sang "Michelle My Belle" to her on the way to Winn Dixie. She laughed and rolled her eyes, "That stuff doesn't work anymore on me, Dad. I'm grown up."

"You're what? Eleven?"

"Twelve now," she said proudly.

Michelle wanted egg-nog for the whole family to share, so I got some, and they did not have the feta cheese I always used, so I bought cottage cheese instead. In my head, I kept trying to figure out if it was noodles-cheese-sauce-meat, or meat-sauce-cheese-noodles, until it became like Algebra. Finally I just told myself to go with the flow. Be spontaneous.

In the grocery store light, as we waited to be checked

through, I felt tingly and sad and full of gladness looking upon my daughter. On the way out we passed by a plastic pink pony you could ride for fifty cents. I asked Michelle if she wanted to ride it.

She laughed. "Dad," she said. "I'm twelve. Didn't you hear me in the car?"

"Yeah. You're right."

I took 500 dollars out of my savings at an ATM on the way home. I decided to give each daughter 250 apiece for Christmas. I was in debt up to my neck, and this withdrawal would deplete my account, but I felt the need. I stuffed the money into my pocket before I walked away from the machine. I knew what I was doing. I saw Michelle in the car, singing along to the radio.

How did you come from me? I asked her mentally. She just kept singing.

We did not use the garage door opener on purpose. We walked through the front door, and the living room was completely lit up with all the decorations. There was a tree that stretched up to the ceiling, cluttered with ornaments, and on every possible surface garland and knickknacks and little bouquets and wreathes.

In the kitchen, Regina, Amber and Irene were smoking together, laughing now. The tension from just an hour or so ago had disappeared, and mixing in with the smell of their mutual smoke was the vapor of baking cookies. Some of the cookies were out of the oven and on the counter cooling: Santa faces and snowmen and gingerbread people.

Regina looked up at me, "We called a truce, Daddy. On your behalf."

"Thanks," I said.

Irene stayed on the chair, inhaling from her Virginia Slim, looking upset still. She was sacrificing her own anger so that all her decorations and cookie-baking would not go to waste.

"The girls explained to me that I had told Amber somewhere in there that I had change for a twenty in my purse, and she was just getting change for a twenty. My mistake." Her smile looked weak and full of pain.

Amber and Regina seemed triumphant. They kissed. Then Regina stood up and stretched. Her heft overtook the kitchen, but her face was rosy with happiness. I loved her then as much as I did Michelle, for reasons too complicated to go into, except it was something about how you can never have what you want, even if you have what you want. This is what you saw when you looked into Regina's big, fat, rosy face.

"What did you guys get?" Regina asked me, looking into the bags.

Michelle went to the counter and smoothed out a space. "Christmas Eve lasagna. Daddy's making it for us, like he used to," she said, very serious.

"Goodie!" Regina said.

"Like my cookies?" Irene said to me.

"Wonderful."

As soon as I started getting down to work, Irene took

out the last batch of cookies to cool. Michelle poured everyone egg-nogs out of the half-gallon carton. My lasagna came out beautifully. We ate in the dining room, with Christmas music on. Amber and Regina fed each other at one point. No one said anything because we were trying to maintain the spirit, and I toasted Darlene's new job. We talked about jobs and money and how this next year was going to be great, especially for Michelle because this summer she was going to go to a music camp in Nashville.

"I play the flute," Michelle said.

"I did not know that," I said.

"She just took it up, but she is so good," Irene said.

Michelle, Irene and I did the dishes. Regina and Amber went back to Regina's room and put on music of their own. Irene just rolled her eyes.

"I am gonna make this work," she said.

As I was turning on the dishwasher, the idea hit me. I turned around and saw Dutchess, on the third step up, looking in at us with sad eyes through the bars of the baby gate.

"Are you sure it's the garage door opener that does it?" I asked.

Michelle was in the living room, getting things ready. We used to always open our gifts on Christmas Eve, except for what Santa brought for the girls. Irene looked over at Dutchess, then back at me.

"Pretty sure. I mean, today I wasn't down in the basement when the opener went off, but I went down there as soon as I heard it, and she was on her back. Poor thing. We keep that gate up so she stays down there. I don't want her pooping all over my new carpet up here."

"Well let's try a little experiment, why don't we? I'll go down to the basement with Dutchess, and I'll yell for you to press the garage door opener button. Then we'll know for sure. You want to?"

Irene laughed, "I guess."

I pulled the baby gate off, walked down. Dutchess got up on her hind legs and started to lick me. She was fine right now.

"Come on girl, come on," I said. I sat on the sofa, and she jumped up beside me. Michelle came down.

"Mom said you were trying something," she said.

I nodded, and then yelled up to Irene, "Go ahead and flick the switch!"

Michelle stood before Dutchess and me. The garage door opener started making a ghost-like hum and then the clank of chains. I held onto Dutchess, afraid, looking into her face. The noise seemed to register in her eyes, like she was remembering some traumatic event. I was holding her and she was breathing hard toward my face, and I thought there for a second she might go into a seizure, but then she licked me and rested on my lap the parts she could. She did not fall to the ground or twitch at all.

Michelle clapped her hands, beaming.

"Let's see now," I said. I felt like a doctor diagnosing a patient. I grabbed Michelle's hand and walked up stairs,

Dutchess following, but I put the gate up so she could not get through.

"Go get me a dog biscuit," I said, and Michelle got one. I threw it down to the basement floor. Dutchess went after it.

"Hey Irene, go ahead and do the garage door again now," I said.

She did so. That same hum-and-chains sound. I could see Dutchess down there beside the sofa. She was beginning to gnaw on the doggie treat, but then as soon as the garage door went off she stopped. She looked up in panic, and she fell to the floor. Twitching commenced.

"She's doing it," I said. "She's doing it."

"Oh no," Michelle said, totally deflated.

"Yeah, she's doing it," I said again. I'd thought I might be able to solve this issue. Be somebody for them.

Irene said, from the doorway to the garage, "You're gonna clean it up."

After cleaning up the mess Dutchess made, and after we did our gift exchange, and we watched some movie on cable, as I was lying on the sofa bed, with Dutchess at my feet, I thought about how my experiment with Dutchess might produce dividends. I tried to figure out a non-pill cure. But that seemed to be impossible. It was about her missing a flesh-and-blood presence in the room, and it seemed to be conscious as well as unconscious. I thought about how people put ticking alarm clocks in with puppies, when they first get them, to quiet their whines and yips from being taken from their mommies. Thought about maybe having a full-sized mannequin (the type they use in mouth-to-mouth training for the Red Cross) set up down here with tape-recorded human breathing connected to it, a heating pad in its lap so Dutchess might crawl up on the mannequin's lap for safety. But I also knew you could not simulate the real thing. Dutchess would know.

Michelle came down the steps with her sleeping bag right when I thought I was ready to go to sleep. She put it on the floor beside the couch-bed, and I told her to be careful where the dog had done its business. She said she knew where it was.

"I wanted to keep you company," she said.

Her nightgown was yellow, her hair damp from a bath. She was so perfect to me. I knew what love was and yet also I knew I could not take it most of the time. It was too much to handle, like you were constantly having to take a cake out of the oven without any oven mitts on. That's the way it was for me, at least.

"Come on up here with me," I said.

She smiled. Climbed into the bed with me. I kissed her cheek and smelled her wet hair.

"Thanks for the money," she said.

"You deserve it. You can use it to buy yourself some summer outfits for music camp," I said.

"Yeah. Thanks. Did you like your cologne?"

"Oh yes I did. Smelled good."

Dutchess yawned at the foot of the bed.

"Poor thing," Michelle said.

"Santa's coming," I said.

"God, Dad. Don't do the Santa thing."

"Well, sorry."

"I'm twelve okay?"

"You can be twelve and believe in Santa."

"If you're retarded."

She laughed and rolled over, and I felt the need to watch her fall asleep.

Michelle had played her flute while we did the gift exchange. She missed several notes. Regina and Amber laughed. In the glow of all of Irene's Christmas lights, though, Michelle seemed to pull apart from her environment, taken away by what she could do, or try to do.

They got me cologne and socks and a Whitman's Sampler, as it had always been a family joke that I have a major sweet tooth. Amber got Regina a Melissa Etheridge sweatshirt and Regina got Amber a pair of sweat-pants. All three girls had gone in together for a gift for Irene, a leather day planner and organizer for her new career, to help her stay more organized for all her home visits. Irene gave Regina and Amber gift certificates to the movies and Olive Garden, and for Michelle she got her a Back Street Boys CD and a pair of Nikes.

We all sat in the living room after the gifts, and that's when I said, "Well I guess you guys are waiting on what I got you."

I took the money out of my pockets. Went over to Michelle and Regina and gave them the cash at the same time.

"Gosh Dad," Regina said, counting it. She got up awkwardly from the sofa and hugged me. Michelle hugged me, and then Irene said, "How much?"

Regina looked shocked, "250 dollars!"

"Gosh, Jerry. Moneybags," Irene said, smiling.

We pushed away all the bad feelings for this one night, and at one point, while Michelle was playing the flute, I almost broke down, almost found myself having to get up and go to the bathroom, but then I wiped my eyes on my sleeves, and this feeling went away.

The next morning, Regina and Irene got into it over pancakes versus waffles. Irene was in her phlebotomist outfit, and Regina was in a big house-robe, Amber sitting off to the side in her new sweat-pants. Michelle was in her room getting dressed. I came into the scene right when Regina said, "Amber wanted waffles. You just do this stuff Mom, you just do this on purpose!"

Irene looked at her then. Her eyes were blazing, "I am not going through this. I am not." She threw the spatula down onto the floor, her face stone-cold, walking past me.

Regina sat down next to Amber, "What did I say?"

Amber slumped her shoulders.

"You guys have a waffle iron?" I said.

I burned the first one, but made waffles. Regina and Amber ate, and Michelle came in and ate and then took

Dutchess out to the big backyard. Dutchess seemed
skittish, afraid to go, but Michelle prodded her. Regina
and Amber went to the video store. As soon as they left,
Irene came out of her bedroom and told me she had to
go draw blood from some people in Kingsport.

"They're on strict schedules, you know, for blood draws,
liver function problems. Anyway somebody has to do it,
even on Christmas day, and you get paid double." She had
put on lipstick, done her hair, to go draw people's blood.

"You like that job?" I asked her, rinsing off a plate.

"It's better than working in a nursing home. You just do
their blood and you're off, you know? You just have to be
real, real careful, about needle pricks and air bubbles and
getting the right vein. I went through a year's training. I
know where almost all the veins are in the human arm."
She smiled at me. "You want me to show you how I do
it?"

I looked at her, "For real?"

"Come here."

I dried off my hands, sat down. She pulled a needle-less
syringe out from her case, and took my left arm into her
hands, delicately pulling out a rubber tie from her pocket
and forming a tourniquet on my upper arm, almost like a
ballet movement. She massaged my veins. It took about
thirty seconds. The vein she found came smoothly to the
surface like a tentacle from the bottom of the sea. She
stuck the needle-less syringe toward it, and pretended to
draw blood slowly out, undid the tourniquet, and placed a
cotton ball where the little prick should have been.

"God, you are a pro," I said.

"You bet," she said. Then she leaned down to me and kissed me on the mouth, saying, "I miss you."

"I miss you too," I said.

She laughed. "Don't lie."

I remembered how when we first dated she used to laugh at everything I said so hard her face would be streaming with tears, and this hysterical laughter had horrified me into thinking that I had to love her. She licked her lips now.

"You really have a girlfriend?"

I nodded.

"Not a boyfriend?"

"No."

She packed up her case and purse. "I thought you'd just go all the way gay after the divorce," she said.

"Oh honey," I said.

"Never mind. I'll be out till five or six I'd say. When's your bus?"

"Four thirty this afternoon," I said. I'd called this morning and that was the only one I could take, to be back tomorrow morning to open up Old Country Buffet.

"Regina and Amber can take you," she said.

I stood up and hugged her. Felt her crush me softly into her.

"Bye bye," she said, and she walked out to her car in the driveway.

I watched Michelle out in the yard running with

Dutchess, and then Regina and Amber came back with
seven or eight movies to watch. I sat in the living room
with all of them, watching *Batman Forever, Aliens,* and *Top
Gun,* until it was time to go. They were all sleepy and
enjoying the holiday, so I told them I would take a cab to
the bus station.

"You sure?" Regina whispered. Amber was asleep,
curled up toward part of Regina's bulk like a small, loving
pet. I was very glad then that Regina had somebody.

"Yeah."

Michelle was on the floor with Dutchess. She got up
and sat on my lap.

"Stay till tomorrow," she whispered.

"Can't honey. Gotta work. Pay the bills."

She started to cry. I did not want to see this. A sudden
burst of anger at her, for crying, crawled into my head. I
fought this off and petted her hair real slow.

Close to one in the morning, we pull into the
Cincinnati depot. Hurt has gotten into my heart, possibly
through that vein Irene had brought up, a deep hurt like I
have abandoned them all over again. In fact, as I stepped
onto the bus earlier in Johnson City, I had half-hoped
that Spider might be picked up somewhere along the
way, through another incident of karma, and we would
talk about how our separate Christmases went. I would
tell him how I was almost happy the girls' gifts had been
stolen while we had done what we did because they really
did seem to enjoy getting the money. How I made a

lasagna and tried to solve the dog problem. Then Spider and I might get together for another little session. That's not love, I know. But it's something, what prevents you from losing your mind, or maybe what helps you to get over love because it hurts like this, this feeling as I get off the bus and my feet are slightly asleep at one AM day after Christmas, and I walk into the depot.

I see Candy right off, waiting. Dressed in jeans and a rabbit-fur coat, pink tennis shoes, her hair shiny blonde, face made up to perfection.

"My baby," she says, hugging me.

Everything moves through moments such as this, the way blood moves through veins. The tiniest amounts of time, one second and you are here wrapped in the perfumed hide of dead rabbits, your girlfriend holding you, kissing the top of your head, and I wonder why she wears fur when she gets all torn up about killing a coyote, but then I erase that thought, and on the way home in the car, she says, "Can't wait for you to see what I got you."

I think of my gift to her, Service Merchandise earrings and bracelet, in the bottom of my underwear drawer. Wrapped by the lady at the store in extremely classy paper. Once we get back home, Candy makes me close my eyes before going in. She walks me down the sidewalk to the steps, and then into the house. Almost as soon as I enter, I smell something sweet, like hay mixing in with the smell of spit.

I open my eyes, and a puppy, small with its eyes still not quite opened all the way, is scratching at the sides of a box lined with paper. The puppy whines, and I look up at Candy's face.

"Isn't he cute?" she says. "I got him from my brother. His Doberman had puppies and she died during childbirth and we have to feed this little thing with a baby-bottle."

Candy picks up the puppy and hands him to me. His eyes are shut, but he is whining and yipping. Through some ugly twist of fate, he has been stolen from where he wants to be and given to people who want him, but still there's something wrong. I hold him like a baby, I cuddle him, I smell him. Candy goes into the kitchen and gets a bottle. She gives the bottle to me. I can't talk. The puppy squirms toward the nipple.

"He's yours," Candy says. "All yours."

What We Ate
That Day
After Church

Fried chicken from the place that used to be Kentucky
Fried Chicken, but they lost the franchise, but they still
kept frying chicken under the name of Country Fried
Chicken. Big bucket of that, with mashed potatoes that
were slightly yellow and brown gravy like stuff left under
an old car but that tasted just as good as anything. Green
beans cooked in bacon fat. Corn on the cob from Alice's
garden, which Alice cooked in a big pot of boiling water
in Momma's kitchen, saying how the pot was not big
enough, and that was why it kept boiling over and putting
the pilot light out, and Momma saying, "We could have
just bought the dern corn on the cob at Kentucky Fried,"
and Alice going, "No, no, it is Country Fried now, not
Kentucky Fried," and Momma laughing at Alice being
particular, "Does that really make a difference in our lives,
Alice?"

Sliced tomatoes from the store because Alice's tomatoes
didn't do too well or at least that's what she was saying,
but we all suspected she was hoarding them because she
was a tomato-holic in secret.

"We got peas?" Daddy asks from the bedroom where he
is trying to put on his tet-hose because Momma yelled at
him. He'll be in there till everything's ready shoving them
things on. "Get some peas from the dad-blamed freezer,"
Momma says because Daddy will not shut up about peas.

Cole slaw because Dale has to have cole slaw with
chicken. "It's like pie without ice cream," he says in the
corner with little Tiffany who has her front tooth missing.

"It's going to be hard for her to eat corn," Tiffany's

mom Pauline says, but nobody listens to Pauline because
she happens to be having an affair. We don't think Dale
knows, but everybody else on God's green earth does, an
affair with some guy who works at the hospital she met
taking a night-class on creative writing at the community
college in Johnson City. She is writing poems all the
time now, secretly reciting them to me and Momma and
even Alice about this guy she met, this guy she named in
poems as Terence, just showing out, a name of Terence
sounding like a made-up As the World Turns name, but
we listen: Terence comes to me/Floating up the stairs
with the face of a statue/And the eyes of a something-
something. We all know what she's doing with them
poems, but we just say, "That's too fancy for our blood."

Macaroni and cheese for Tiffany and my two boys as
they always like that, plus Momma makes the best, and
I have brought along with me some of that broccoli
casserole left-over, which my husband Randy says doesn't
look good bringing leftovers, and I tell him, "We ain't
visiting the Kennedys, Randy," and Randy says, "If it was
your family, my dear, you would not only make a brand
new dish of that broccoli stuff, but you would also have
put it on your silver plate," and I say, "What silver plate are
you referring to Randall?" "The one in the kitchen," he
says. "Oh that silver plate," I say, but then again he is okay
for someone who works nights.

Our two boys get worked up over the chocolate pie
Momma makes and the strawberry pies from Country
Fried which are famous around Johnson City, Kingsport,

and Bristol. Then to drink for all of us we have Pepsi of course and other cheaper store-pop and iced tea with sugar and lemons, and Momma hates it with lemons. She says she does not understand lemons except in lemon-custard. Out of custard, they make her nervous.

Momma, Randy's mom, not mine, but she makes me call her Momma, and I don't really care either way, Momma tells me while I put the chicken out on the table that Dale is looking pretty peaked over there in the corner by that floor-lamp he was telling her he was going to fix, and then we look over at Pauline who is sitting watching TV all by her lonesome.

"Well, I really feel sorry for her," I whisper to Momma, smart-aleck me, but then I also feel kind of two-faced. Randy takes the boys outside to play something.

Little Tiffany comes into the kitchen and says to Alice, "I'm hungry," and Alice, big old tub of lard that she is, tells Tiffany to scoot that she'll get to feed her little face just as soon as she says so, and Tiffany gets mad and cross, the way hyperactives do. She looks around and then that's it: the green beans are on the floor and she's crying, and there's Pauline coming in and Dale too.

Pauline goes to Tiffany and holds her, she always has been overprotective, and she says, "What happened, baby? Baby?" And Dale says that she could have hurt herself in here why wasn't Pauline watching her? And Pauline says that Tiffany was with Dale for goodness sakes, and he was watching her, and Dale says, "You make me sick!"

Which of course is all out of proportion. Then he is

going over, and he grabs Tiffany, but Pauline knocks his hands away.

Alice says, "Tiffany is the one who did this to herself, hyper-thing."

"Alice," I say, "Just pay attention to your damn corn."

Then Pauline looks at all of us, looks and looks.

"I am not Hester Prynne!" Pauline lets out, and I'm sorry but who in the hell is that?

She walks off like an actress, holding Tiffany's hand. She says later she ain't hungry. "Well boo hoo hoo," says Alice.

I almost forgot. For dessert we also had banana pudding and the brownies with the crushed pecans on top.

Holding Hands for Safety

That night Trent, my cousin, came over, he did not act like anything. Just kind of lounged around the living room of our apartment like the god of beauty he must've thought he was, or would always be, all five foot, seven inches of him, with his bleached-out crew cut and public-pool tan and the easy, confident grin of a shark in a cartoon.

His glass of Pepsi, though, the one I got him without him asking, shook when he brought it up to his mouth. His eyes were swollen and red. He could not really "lounge," either, as much as shake his legs and drink nervously from his glass, every so often commenting on what I was watching on the VCR, which happened to be *Mad Max Beyond Thunderdome*.

"This is pure grade-A shit, Clyde," he might say. Or: "Borrrrring."

Me, I just thought it was drugs.

I just thought, Great, Mom and Freddy are gone, so it's just me and Trent. And Trent was on drugs, which might mean he might let me you-know with him. Might allow me the privilege — who knows? There is always hope in little hearts. Sometimes Trent would get pissed right in the middle and kick me away. I'd kick him right back, and we'd start fighting, and the fighting would lead back into what we were doing in the first place. I was only sixteen, and he was all of eighteen. People were always asking him, "Why don't you join the army, Trent-O," or "Why don't you go to trade school," or "Why don't you at least get a job and help your mom, who you happen to

be bloodsucking off of." He answered back almost always
with the same poem — him holding his crotch, sticking
his middle finger into his mouth, pulling it out of his
mouth slow and showing it wet.

So, like I was saying, he did not really act like anything
had happened that night. Quiet as hell mostly, sitting
there, any other night. That grin coming out when he
said something smart-assed, then closing down. I crawled
over to him about a half-hour into his stay, sat up beside
his legs, as he was sitting in Freddy's La-Z-Boy chair, the
one no one was supposed to sit in but Freddy ("I have got
one rule and one rule only..."). Big fat Freddy was Mom's
latest boyfriend, a little older than her, and he worked at
the hospital in maintenance. Trent and him could get
along enough to hunt deer.

I am sitting on the floor next to Trent's hairy legs,
watching *Mad Max*, Tina Turner wearing a screen door,
and I look up at him. I expect him to pretend to spit at
me or maybe even fucking do that. But suddenly Trent
slides down the chair onto the floor right beside me. He
waits a second. Then just starts kissing me.

The front door was open, the screen letting in night
noises, brakes going out, car axles bumping up over speed
bumps, kids screaming, sometimes a bash of head or fist
against concrete. I imagine what the ignorant and the
small-minded neighbors we got in this complex would
think: bleach-blond crew-cut high-school graduate with
no future french-kissing his cousin, the black-headed,
slightly overweight sixteen-year-old boy who works part-

time at Burger King on Pleasant Avenue and tells people
he gets good grades when he is only but average (if even
that).

Kissing, this time, Trent used tongue and teeth. Now
usually it was a quick peck and then down to business.
That was okay, but this kissing was like it was being
videotaped for the Kissing Channel. He had his whole
mouth wide open, and I tasted the sourness of a sore
throat starting, a storm brewing way off, the bruised
goodness of his warm breath like something overripe kept
in a hot kitchen out on the counter. I kissed back deep.
We did this for about five minutes approximately before I
got up to breathe and to shut the door.

I did not say one thing. Did not want to ruin my good
luck.

Trent stayed on the floor. He did not really look that
incredibly horny. He looked tired, stupid, beautiful, and
something I had not seen before in his arrogant ass: he
looked scared. Scared-shaken like a dog gets and you
don't know what to do. Dogs are not supposed to be
scared, right? I leave all the lights off. I close the curtains,
turn the sound down on the TV.

I sat down beside him again. This time he got up.
Turned around and looked at me.

"I killed Courtney," he says. Then he laughs like it is
just so unbelievable.

Courtney was his little half-sister. They did not have
the same daddy. Trent, Courtney, and their mom, my
mom's sister, lived in the same apartment complex as us,

as this was one of the few that took Section 8. Borderline retarded, Courtney was tiny and had stringy brown hair and always wore dirty sundresses in the summer. Ten and still shitting herself almost every other day. She'd always be running around the complex, poop stains leaking out the back of her sundress. Always too excited playing, it seemed, to go inside to the toilet. Talking and babbling a lot, and although she was borderline retarded, she had the same exact obnoxious ways of all ten-year-old girls in dumpy apartment complexes, a sort of stupid ass but frilly pride that made her talk back to people in a high pitch and paint her toenails out on the sidewalk like a show and wear lip gloss from her mom's purse and throw rocks at parked cars and steal all the mail flyers from the shelf under the locked boxes up front, throwing them around and into the air like birds getting caught in a jet propeller.

"I just killed Courtney," Trent repeats, still laughing in disbelief. He can't say nothing else, coming over to me, swooping down like Batman. I ain't believing it, of course. It's another dumb-ass game of his, a way to trick me.

But he looks at me close then, saying, "She's in the dumpster, Clyde."

(He calls me Clyde because I look like a Clyde he once knew. My actual name is Brian.)

Then Trent laughs again. This time though with sadness leaking out of his closed teeth as he does it, the sadness like a crazy voice in a shut garage. Then he stands up and goes down the hall to where my bedroom is.

I laugh too. It is kinda funny: Courtney, Little Miss Retard Big-mouth, her panties full of shit, dead in the dumpster. I mean, some things vulgar and sick like that can often be funny, like Marilyn Manson or Howard Stern or *Pink Flamingos*. But still there wasn't any reality to it right then, that was the main reason I could laugh.

Or maybe it is just some things, no matter how serious, how dumb and serious, you have to laugh at or you lose your mind.

Plus all I was thinking right now was how Trent had gone down to my bedroom. I mean, "butterflies" was not the word for what was in my stomach. Fucking Steven Spielberg pterodactyls. Trent was in there getting into my bed. Like he loved me.

But for a second I just stood there, shocked, contemplating my good fortune, looking at the godforsaken brown vinyl couch, the spools for electric cable Mom had painted and antiqued to turn into end tables, the shelves filled with Mom's romance novels and my horror and sci-fi ones, the TV screen with *Mad Max* still going on it a little fuzzy, Freddy's big tiger picture framed in chrome he bought as his gift for Mom letting him stay here...

I take a deep breath of all the air we usually breathe, stale and corn-chippy and like all our feet have left a smell combining into Family capital F: thinking of family and what me and him were about to do, and then too about Courtney. Was she dead? Of course not. It was Trent's sick sense of humor. I thought of Courtney in a flash,

how one time she begged and begged me to walk with
her to the store because she had a food-stamp dollar she
found in the kitchen drawer. How she stood in front of
me while I was watching I think it was *Hellraiser 3*, me
getting pissed, but then I finally got up.

"Jesus Christ, okay," I told her.

And she wanted me to hold her hand. This time the
sundress was orange with pink straps. She looked at me
as I got my shoes on, and she said, "We got to hold hands.
Mom said. For safety."

I kind of laughed at her, tying my shoes. Her mom
did not give a shit about holding hands for safety. Still,
though, I let it go. She was fresh form her bath and clean
and kind of sweet, her stringy hair still dark with water.

"Come on," I told her.

I took her hand. It was very warm, like inside she was
always hot, always "on."

We walked together. It was one of those half-rainy days,
still hot though. She pulled on me, and I tried not to be
mad at her because she was borderline retarded and hyper.
I tried, but soon I let go of her hand and told her to go
on by herself. Told her to get lost. I wanted to finish
Hellraiser.

"You get lost!" she screamed. But she ran on ahead.

I turned back, went home. Later I saw that she had got
Reese's Cups with her food-stamp dollar. She ate them
both off by herself, over by where the chain-link fence
started, by the back woods. She was still pissed at me.
Sitting there outside.

Now I hear Trent from back there, the back bedroom where I sleep.

"Come on," Trent says. "What the fuck are you waiting for, fag?"

I can tell by his voice he is lying down.

I go.

He is in my bed, naked, not muscular, just skinny, but him not having muscles makes him prettier. He has never got all-the-way naked before. My face turns red and hot, and I stand there. He looks up at me, just the sheet over the bottom part of his legs. He needs me, it looks like — needs me like he has not needed me, or maybe anybody, before. Like I am his version of safety. This scares me back and gets me suspicious, but I cannot pass him up, of course.

"Come on," he whispers. His eyes are shiny. He has a little-kid face, a little kid who wants something but he cannot tell you because it's embarrassing.

"Get in bed here," he says. He strains his voice. "Honey," he goes.

The next morning, of course, Trent is gone, because we don't want my mom or Freddy knowing what we do. Alone, I rise feeling all elegant. There is that specialness to waking up after getting exactly what you want and not having to explain it to nobody. This one hundred-percent-pure happiness. That's kind of what I liked about living here and being sixteen and being gay. Oh sure, eventually I would get sick of hiding it and have to run away maybe to San Francisco or somewhere I don't know, but right now the secrecy of it is what makes it so special. So original. That and this afterglow feeling and not having to explain it to a soul. My own secret world inside my head after getting what I want. Still naked, I held my gut in as I stepped into my clothes angelically.

I know I had a smile on, cruising down the short hall toward the living room, where Mom and Freddy were already up.

There on the morning news was a picture of Courtney.

Mom says, in her frayed-out housecoat, "She didn't come home last night, Brian." It was one of those serious whispers she gets when she wants to show how terrible things are. But in reality I saw her the way she would kick Courtney's little ass out of the apartment and the way too she talked about how Courtney needed somebody there to discipline her because Peggy — who was on disability for her back — was too damn lazy for raising kids. Plus Dean, Courtney's dad, was in jail for writing bad checks.

But now, with Courtney's picture on the TV, Mom was all feeling about it.

Freddy goes, "Wipe that stupid grin off your face."

I guess I was still smiling. From satisfaction at first, then from shock. I wiped it off.

"All the news programs have showed up, because Peggy called the police at five this morning. I was trying to wake you up but you had your door locked. I swear you sleep like a damn corpse. I guess the TV people watch the police scanner for situations like this," Mom goes.

Then on the TV is Peggy, who lived four buildings down. There she is in predawn light on her patio which overlooks the high school and the front of the complex. Peggy in a big t-shirt, no bra, her hair graying out from her black dye job, her mouth un-lipsticked, eyes baggy.

"I don't know where she could have gone. I called everybody that I could," Peggy says on the TV. There is this picture of police taking down information from neighbors in the complex.

What the hell am I thinking? Of course what Trent told me. I stand there, and Freddy says, "Peggy has let her go unsupervised way too much. You don't know what kind of trouble a girl like her can get into. The freaks out there who pick little girls up and..."

Mom bursts into tears.

"I am going over there right now!" she screams. She goes into the bedroom and comes back out with a pair of old sneakers and socks and sits down on the couch to put them on angrily, like she is going against what Freddy has told her. That is their relationship: him laying down the law, her going against the law but also not a lot of the time so mostly it's just him and her getting along smashingly. Which is all Mom has ever wanted from her men: a smashingly successful relationship. Do not ask me about my dad, who lives in Kentucky or Tennessee and is a truck driver and sends me twenty-dollar Sears gift certificates for Christmas.

"Dorothy, you go over there now and you ain't gonna

be able to help her no how," Freddy says, in his chair, in his work uniform, white pants and white shirt and black shoes. Maybe it's that he is jealous of Peggy, that Peggy and Courtney are getting all the attention. He has the biggest head, like a mongoloid, and yet he doesn't look retarded. He looks like a big white genius, even though I know mostly he is a stupid racist asshole who when he gets drunk sometimes brags about the KKK and hunting niggers like deer. But then on TV he watches Cosby and Urkel reruns and laughs and even has a black friend at work named Roy. Roy and him go drinking sometimes.

Mom slides her feet into her shoes hard.

"I am going, Freddy."

"Fine," Freddy says. "I gotta go to work anyways. Go over there and bother her. Go on. That's what you're good for. Get your goddamn picture on TV."

"You can shut your mouth right now," Mom says, standing up, and then she looks at me.

"They are gonna have a search party," she says. "You go get dressed and you go with me, you hear? Thank God you finally woke up, Sleeping Beauty."

Her face, that serious, desperate mascara-eyed face with its blonde curly hair and black eye-brows and those double chins, I want to slap it for some reason. Then I see Trent in my head, his face so alive as he came while I was jerking him off.

I felt perverted, I felt stupid, but the secrecy came back. No one would know anything anyways, right? So the beautiful secrecy of what we had done before and did last night comes back to me, like someone opened a door and right outside that door was Saturn spinning closer and closer till it gets in through my eyes into my brain.

"Get in there and get dressed. Get you a Pop-Tart," Mom tells me, fat in her pink housecoat and black sneakers and big tube socks. Caring about my breakfast.

"You got to work today?

"Yeah, I have to be in at two," I tell her.

"Well, that's three hours anyways. Get dressed."

Freddy is grunting, sitting up out of his chair. He comes over to me.

"You sit in my chair?" he asks me.

It pisses me off, how accurate Freddy can predict stuff. Like his ass has telepathy.

"No."

"Who did?"

"Trent," I blurt out. I walk back to my room and get dressed slowly, and then I hear him say, "You tell Trent to keep his lazy ass out of my chair, you got it?"

"Yeah," I yell back, through the shut door.

Then Freddy leaves, and I come out in my Nikes, t-shirt, and cut-off sweat pants. Feeling dirty form the sex last night but also liking the glazed fishy quality of it all over my body. Like I am trying to prolong what me and Trent did. Then I picture Courtney like I had done last night: in a dumpster. Dead.

I need to tell Mom what Trent told me. I need to. But don't have to.

Mom gives me a packet of those watermelon Pop-Tarts

I had her get. I bite into one as we walk out into the
hot sun. It tastes so sweet my teeth start to ache right
off. There are still TV trucks and vans here. It makes you
wonder why anyone would care about old Courtney
anyways? Some retarded white-trash girl with an
unnerving face and shit-stained sundress throwing rocks?
I mean, she isn't Princess Diana, obviously. But they are
lined up to report on finding her, like she has fallen down
a well. Like her life meant anything.

Serious business, all them white vans and trucks with
big primary-colored logos on them (CHANNEL 13
ACTION NEWS— WE CARE; CHANNEL 6, YOUR
AWARD-WINNING 24-HOUR LOCAL NEWS
STATION, etc.). Satellites, police cars, all surrounding
Peggy and Trent and Courtney's apartment. Trent's
Chevette, yellow with a WIBN frog-mouth sticker on it,
ain't out there. I am walking beside Mom, like we are in
war-torn Bosnia.

Mom says to me, "Trent is gone. Ain't that just like
him? Leaving right when he is needed. Courtney is his
sister."

"Half-sister," I say, not thinking, eating the goddamn
Pop-Tart, gagging on it.

Mom just looks at me in bewilderment.

"Some people are saying he did something to her,"
Mom whispers as we walk.

I realize at this point that I am involved in a conspiracy.
Trent told me because he knew he could trust me, did
he not? He told me then let me have my way with

him because he had to tell somebody. Plus he needed someone to love him right after he told them. Like religion, like being saved. He knew that I would not tell no one because I wanted him so bad, and that makes me feel trashy but also full of hope again because it will only be me and him who know.

It is so damn hot and sticky, the sky above the complex smoggy from the interstate. I finish my second Pop-Tart as we go past the police cars.

A policeman is standing outside the apartment.

Mom goes, "Peggy Stewart is my sister. I need to see her."

The policeman has a big mustache and a gut and he stands back not saying nothing.

"This is my son, Brian. He is going to help with the search party."

Mom smiles, all take-charge and shit. I remember when I was six, and Dad had left. It was just me and Mom in the kitchen on a bright winter's day. She held me out of school, and she got blitzed, sat me down at the dinette set. In her bra and her panties, she said to me these speeches of bizarre gut-wrenching sadness that did not make any sense. Just like she was talking to some adult who could pity her for being so fried she couldn't put two sentences together.

Now she was with AA. Now she had Freddy to keep her ass in line.

Peggy was in her living room, looking doped up. There was a couple of other fat women, neighbors, and also a

blond and thin reporter in a professional skirt outfit with
a microphone, a tall cameraman in a t-shirt and jeans
behind her. One of the obese ladies was holding Peggy's
hand, one of those instant friends you get when you go
through a real glamorous tragedy like losing your kid. You
could tell by Mom's face she was hurt, that she thought
she should be the one on camera holding Peggy's hand.
If Freddy had not held her back, she could have been the
one holding her sister's hand on TV.

The blond woman had that husky, reporter way of
speaking. It was not live, it was being taped for the noon
edition, the other obese lady whispered to Mom and me.

"So, Peggy, when does the search party begin?" said the
professional reporter.

Peggy says, "Soon as everyone gets here." In a spooked
victim voice. "It's so nice. All these people."

Positioned by the front door, I saw some kids coming
from beyond the front buildings, men and women too.
Neighbors you don't talk to really, just pass by on your
way to work or school, but here they were showing up to
find a little girl no one liked.

Mom says then, interrupting, "I am Peggy's sister. I just
live down the way there. I think what's happened is that
Courtney just forgot to tell her mom, and as soon as she
wakes up or one of her friends sees it on TV, they'll call."

Mom smiles, like she knows deep in her heart.

The cameraman doesn't turn the mini-cam on her, and
people in the room just act like what she said was nothing.

* * *

Peggy and Mom, though, get together after the
interview. Peggy bursts into tears and Mom does too.
The other people let the sisters have their time together. I
notice people I know, people I don't, all of them pulling
together in this desperate time of need.

I wondered where Trent was hiding.

When we passed that mustached policeman I thought
of just telling him. Thought of saying that Trent told me
he killed Courtney and put her in the dumpster. I mean,
when we went to bed together last night he did not
mentioned anything else, not even after, and I just let it
slide, but I was an accomplice now. And that almost had a
beautiful sound to it.

All this searching was a lost cause, people. I was a
know-it-all.

We got organized outside little Courtney's apartment,
and we searched.

I thought about going to that dumpster by the back
of their building first thing. It has a brick encasement
around it, brown, big as a grand piano, the lid shut tight.
But I didn't. I got caught up in the search. It was like an
Easter-egg hunt, people walking around, yelling her name.
Some going across the way toward the big ditch, some
in the parking lot of the high school, some down a hill
toward the water tower.

I walked around and called her name too, feeling foolish
but also part of something important. Mom and Peggy

sat outside the front door of Peggy's apartment, like the
queen of tragedy and her tragic sister, two of them ruling
over this little colony of searchers. I walked in the grass
and looked in the weeds and in the trees, knowing that
inside the brown dumpster was where she was. Finally,
after an hour, I got so sweaty and stupid with the hunt,
and with the feeling that I was all the way completely evil,
that I walked over toward the dumpster where they lived.

I heard my mom say, "What are you doing?" Still sitting
there on the lawn chair next to Peggy, supervising.

"I just thought I'd look," I said, not turning my head
around. I felt my stomach go out of my body like it had
been raised up and levitated out of my eyes. I was caught.
Why had he killed her? This hit me, as I stood there.
What was the fucking point? She was just some dumb
little girl. Right there staring at the brown dumpster with
the rusty door handles, I felt so stupid with sorrow that I
did not want to see nothing, not her body, not her face.

Mom says, "Look where?" She comes over to me, fast.
"In the dumpster?" she whispers. Her breath smells of old
damp cigarettes.

"Yeah."

I am shaky, like a diabetic. I have had too much sugar.
I need some insulin. Freddy is diabetic, and he does his
own shots like a junkie in the bathroom. Talking real loud
the whole way through, stupid bull-shit, because he says
talking real loud gets him over the fear of needles he has.

"No, don't look in there," Mom says. Like it would be
in bad taste somehow. Her face loses its seriousness and

gets a silly absurd expression, like no way no one could
do that to a little girl, kill her and put her in a dumpster.
No one would do that. But then I thought of that one
time Freddy brought home a big deer on his car hood
and then out in the goddamn parking lot he cuts the
damn thing's head off with a saw and brings the head
into our apartment and boils the head in a pot of water
in the kitchen. The smell was not of this earth, hot and
coppery and tangy like a chemical spill, singeing into your
face and eyes and nose. He wanted to make the skull into
a sculpture to be hung on a wall. "A European mount"
is what he called it. He threw the parts he did not want
into the dumpster, did he not? But then again Courtney
wasn't a deer, was she?

"Mom, she could be in there," I say, hot gray sun in
my face, her smell of cigarette breath and old sleepy
housecoat, stale and yeasty like grocery-store bread.

"She ain't," says my mom.

"She could be," I say.

I start walking over to the dumpster again. She grabs
my arm. I pull away. I open the door. Four or five big
black birds scatter. Inside, cushioned on white bags of
trash, not even hid by them really, is her.

She was in a nightgown, and her neck was bruised. Her
eyes were open to look out at where she was. Her mouth
was bloody from coughing up blood. Her skin had the
color of that sky above us, hot and cold both at once,
gray-hot, gray-cold, her body puffed out from the heat,
and she was not funny, she was not funny to me, and I did

not cry and I did not laugh.

Mom was behind me.

She sobbed out. Her cries were great big, and I remembered her yelling at Courtney one day when Courtney came in without knocking into our apartment. "Who do you think you are, you little bitch? You knock. You hear me? Did somebody tell you this is your apartment? This ain't your apartment to run in and out of. You hear me?"

Mom doing that in front of Freddy to show Freddy that she could mean business too. But Freddy told Mom to calm the fuck down. Freddy took Courtney into his lap, because Courtney was crying at Mom's display. Freddy smelled her, though. She had done it on herself, of course. Freddy had this look of betrayal upon his face.

"Go on and change yourself, sweetie," he said, putting her down.

Courtney just ran off.

I call off work at Burger King. I have the excuse of being in shock, being the one who found my half-cousin in a dumpster dead like the deer Freddy cut the head off of. The reporters came over once we found her. Mom said she was the one who really saw her first, which might be true. She was the one who talked to the police, telling them it was her who found her because I told her I could not handle it and she already knew I was a kind of an emotionally messed-up kid.

I stayed with Mom for a while after the ambulance

came, after all the people went away. Stayed with Peggy
who had gone into shock too, of course.

Peggy said, her eyes glazed over, "Where's Trent?"

"Nobody knows," Mom says.

"Where is he?" Peggy says, like she did not hear Mom.

Nobody knew. Not even me. And I did not say
nothing to nobody. Everybody was talking, though.
Called him names. I wondered if he had left his
fingerprints on her neck.

"You don't think..." Peggy starts, her eyes zombie-like.
Big and empty.

"I'm beginning to," Mom said back.

They talked about how Trent had always treated
Courtney like his own personal little-girl slave and how
sometimes he would hit her on the head real hard, as a
joke.

"Jokes can get out of hand," Mom, in her all her infinite,
housecoat wisdom, said.

Peggy was too sick and tired to listen to her. She closed
her eyes and opened them, but looked like she was staring
into a volcano.

Soon I just went home, leaving Mom at Peggy's, and as
soon as I got back I collapsed on my bed in my room and
flipped through some old Clive Barker novel I'd read last
summer. Then I remembered last summer, the first time
Trent had come over to our apartment after Dean, his
step-dad, had been sent to jail, and him and his mom and
Courtney had moved in here close to us.

That first time Trent was over, my mom and Freddy

were gone off to the horse races in Kentucky, so it was just me and him. He was bored, and he had pot.

I had loved him since I knew how to love people. Trent, who I loved since I was seven maybe, in the little-boy way of looking up to him, wanting to kiss him even then. Trent, who never paid attention to me never, but then he let me take a toke that night.

"I didn't know you smoked, Clyde," he said. Last year he was not a crew-cut dyed blond, but had longer, dirty-blond hair shaved on top, with strands hanging down off his neck. He had a major tan, though. No shirt on. I was breathless when he arrived. Funny how easy it is to lose yourself, but really I wanted to be lost. I guess everybody does.

"I smoke," I say, letting my lungs let go of it.

"Hey," he says then, taking another toke. He breathes it in like it is the nectar of the gods. He looks at me and laughs at his own pleasure. I take in his laugh as something we are sharing, he is letting us share, and the laugh becomes ours. I taste the hickory leftovers of the pot in my mouth and feel the pot eat into my thoughts like tickling little mice mouths.

"Hey," he says again, relaxing onto the floor. At this time, Freddy's chair wasn't here. Relaxing, shirtless on the floor, Trent grins.

"Are you a fag?" he says. "I mean, I heard you were."

The question did not even hurt my feelings, because I have been called that a lot at school and here. Even if I wasn't, I would still be called that from the way I look. I

don't act like a fairy, I don't think, but I have the look in
my eyes of someone who likes things way too much. It
is that look they are labeling "fag," I'm sure. The fact that
I can't hide how much I want things. But right then, still
drunk off the sound of his pot laugh, I go:

"Who wants to know?"

Trent laughs more. He pulled down his cutoffs slightly,
just to show the start of his pubic hair. I am shaking from
the desire of him. Remembering family cookouts at dusk
with him being thirteen and me being eleven and him the
center of all attention, arm-wrestling all the deadbeat dads
and eating all the potato salad and all the moms getting
pissed at him and him charming them right back into
giving him brownies.

"I do, fag," says Trent then. "Me. I want to know."

I see the way his small belly goes under his underwear
and cutoffs. My mouth is open. I don't even care that
Mom might be able to smell the pot when she gets back.
I go for it because that is who I am.

It was close to sundown when I sat up, and there in my
room, just sitting on the floor, the door closed, was Trent.
The Trent who had killed Courtney just yesterday, that
Trent.

I thought he was a vision, something I had cooked up,
but he was sitting on the floor Indian-style, his eyes wide
open.

"You awake?" Trent said. He smiled with kindness. He
was a changed man. He was a little boy all over again, this

little sweet boy hiding from his mommy and daddy.

"I snuck in," he said.

"How?" I said, getting up.

"Through the front door," he said. "I just like ran in. I left my car at the Shell station on the corner. I didn't know where else to go. I heard they found her."

He was just half-talking-half-whispering, sitting there. His face was peaceful, not scared like last night. Peaceful from drugs or peaceful from insanity, I was not sure.

"I found her," I said, standing up then and walking to him. "Me and Mom did."

"I thought so," he said. He looked up at me and grinned. "Fucking traitor," he says, laughing nervously.

I sat back down on my bed, and he sat beside me on the bed. He was tender, like once you kill a little girl you can allow yourself the luxury of not being macho no more. Not being the guy who gives the finger to passers-by, you can be this weird, fucked-up boy in the same clothes as yesterday, five-o'clocked-shadowed, sitting on the bed next to your gay sixteen-year-old cousin. Maybe you are gay too, but gay and a child killer, so you are no longer that much of a human being. You are this dumb-ass demon, this shadowy thing, this ghost of a person. I loved the ghost, I think, almost more than I loved the real thing.

But there was pity mixed in with it. Pure pity. And also this new thing I had not ever known around Trent: a hatred and a disgust, which only made the love feel deeper.

"She was on the phone yesterday morning and Mom

was at work and I had to call somebody 'cause we were
going out that night," Trent says to me now. Right beside
me. He has to tell.

"She wouldn't get off the fucking phone. She wasn't
even talking to nobody real, the little retard," he says, but
even calling her names did not seem bad, because he
always did that anyways, all the time, when she was alive.
She would hit him back and yell at him, which tickled
anybody who saw her do it: some scrawny little pigtailed
girl trying to beat up on him.

"She was just pretending to talk to someone and just
carrying on, you know."

Trent imitates her. Holds up an invisible phone to
his ear, goes borderline-retarded-little-girl in the face,
babbling in this high voice, "Yes ma'am we do have that in
stock. Yes ma'am I can have that out to you tomorrow."

Trent laughs, "She was fucking playing Service
Merchandise or something. I needed to call my friend
about what was up that night. I tell Courtney to get off
the phone at least ten times, but she won't."

His face gets mad and he is staring off into outer space
then. It's like something that happens a million times,
his killing her. He is seeing her on that phone being
stubborn, and his anger unveils itself like a big trombone
that he is going to blow into, shiny and shaped strange.
He sits there, and gets that pissed-off face back and he
stands up and he says, "You fucking bitch get off the
goddamn phone you ain't even using! You're playing!"

He starts crying but he stops. He goes on.

"And so I grab her and fling her onto the couch. She starts screaming bad. I grab her around the neck, Clyde, and I lift her up to the ceiling. Up there man. She squirms and like just doesn't fucking shut up and then I hear her neck goddamn crack."

He stops. No crying, no anger left. He stops himself from putting on a further show. He climbs back onto my bed, and he looks at me again. He eyes flash out of themselves, and I can tell he doesn't understand totally that what he did is wrong. All he knows is he will be caught, and that is what is making him scared and peaceful both at the same time. Nobody ever liked her anyway, right?

But now everybody loves her. Even me.

I stood up. I go, "Her eyes were open, Trent. When I opened the door. To the dumpster. You should have shut her eyes, man."

He lies back, like he's sick, resting his head on my pillow. He can't say nothing for a second, like he is thinking of those eyes, hers, open. Eyes that look at him and he knows exactly who he is. Eyes that make him want to kill her all over again.

"I know," he says. "I know that."

We don't do anything, except kiss.

I can't do anything else, but this kissing is scary and beautiful, his mouth ripe from being bitten into over and over, his breath really bad but even that is beautiful. I don't think he snuck into my room to do it as much as to tell me it all so that he could go on. He was going to make his run for it soon.

He got up from my bed and he stretched after we kissed. I got up and stood by the closet, standing there, dumb and scared and hating him, but also loving him that way I always had because no matter what he did that love protected him in my eyes, even while I saw Courtney's open eyes, her eyes open and seeing the world for the first time for what it was.

He yawned. A murderer can yawn, I thought. A murderer's got feelings.

"So you telling?" he asks, like it's some prank he pulled.

"I don't know," I say.

"You found her, so if you tell they could get you on something I bet," he says, his voice going back into its middle-finger meanness.

"Yeah," I say. "But I think they already think you did it anyways."

Trent comes up to me. "It was an accident," he says. "I fucking have thrown her against like cement walls, man, and she bounces right off."

When he kisses me that last time, I think of Courtney. I think of three ambulance guys pulling her out of a dumpster, and then I remember how she used to like have this old Operation game she'd play with by herself on the front stoop — you know, the game where you pull out the bones from some guy with a red light bulb for a nose, with electronic tweezers. If you hit the sides, it buzzes. Courtney made the thing buzz on purpose, buzzing out there all day long. I seem them pulling her dead white body out, and I feel myself shaped from that pulling.

Trent pulls back and I miss his mouth automatic.

Mom is out in the living room, because suddenly I hear the TV. Shock brings me back to life.

"Go out through the window," I say.

"You ain't telling?"

"Go out the window," I say.

He does. The screen takes a little time to get off because they painted over the hinges, but finally it falls to the ground outside. He slips out, then turns back and reinstalls the screen, which is stupid but he does it. I see his face while he screws it back. He is stupid and he is beautiful and he is lost. Maybe somehow he is looking forward, in a way, in a sick way, to being hunted down.

My stomach has the empty feeling. I won't ever see him this way again. This close.

He does not say anything else. He goes. Disappears into the woods behind the complex.

I go past Mom in the living room.

"Peggy may be put up on charges," Mom says. It is that same serious voice. She is in her smock from the grocery store. She is tired and curled up on the couch. Maybe she has abandoned her sister.

"They may get her for neglect," Mom adds, and she starts to cry slowly. I stand in front of her, wanting to run away.

"They think that Trent done it," she goes, still crying.

On TV right then: a picture of the ambulance guys pulling her out.

I go outside, ignoring her.

There are candles lit by the dumpster where we found her. There are stuffed toys and flowers hanging off the dumpster's sides in plastic sacks, stuck there with duct tape, and big pieces of paper with her name on them, and cardboard with curlicues and "WE LUV YOU!!! REST IN PEACE DEAR SWEET COURTNEY."

People are standing by the dumpster, people who probably don't even know her, or who when they did would run away from her. It seems like another sick joke, that dumpster fucking decorated for her, like it was her coffin or something. But people usually don't get jokes this serious.

I stand back, a little ways off. A fat retarded man is standing in the candlelight, maybe he is not retarded, who knows? He has on dirty clothes and he speaks in a strange lispy stutter, holding a big Bible. People are both scared of him and listening to him. They wonder where he has come from. He looks like he is out of his mind suddenly, standing there, buzzed-headed with big eyes and a thick-lipped mouth.

"Oh dear Courtney," he says in his way. "Dear sweet little angel! Dear dead Courtney, what has the world come to? Why?"

He reads from the Bible, reads a verse: "'Blessed are the children... Blessed are the meek...'"

He stands there and people laugh, but seriously. He

drops the Bible to the ground then, this freak, and he starts speaking in tongues. Babbling like an idiot, his face jerking, his mouth wide open, letting out the bull-shit of God. Her name comes out of his mouth sometimes, inside all the gibberish.

I see Courtney with her eyes wide open, looking out at what people did, what people do, see her looking at me and then at them. Her eyes are almost crossed but shining like stars that have the ability to read minds. She is reaching out to grab my hand. She wants my stupid hand.

The fat guy opens his eyes then, stopping his tongue-speaking. He is deadly serious, looking at me, then looking at the others, but it seems like he has me targeted, or maybe it's just my paranoia.

"We're all gonna pray now," he says. It is an order.

Leon

Tom Cruise asks me, "What's it like? I mean, Gary, you know, really?"

He does not flash his superstar smile. He is serious, this guy. Dustin Hoffman's across the hall, by the way, watching somebody get their Attends changed. The smell of shit is totally close, and Tom says, "I mean working here?"

There are other people standing around, handlers, security, assistants. A lot of khaki, a lot of leather, a lot of expensive athletic shoes. They aren't going to film anything, just do "research," here at this facility for the mentally retarded. 32 make this place their home, and none of them can talk, except for Leon, and even he has a hard time saying hello and what he wants for supper.

"It's a job," I say.

Tom laughs, saying, "Who's your favorite?"

A guy in a black suit-coat and jeans, with a shaved head, comes over and whispers into Tom's ear.

"Damn, really?" Tom says to this man.

Tom looks at me again, "We're leaving in like ten minutes."

"Leon," I say.

Tom goes, "What?"

"Leon's my favorite."

"Well Leon it is."

I say follow me, like you know the dumb-ass ugly servant in an old-fashioned horror movie, in a haunted castle, Walk this way master......

Leon's head is huge, filled with water, just about twice the normal size, and he has a hard time keeping his face up. There's this shunt in the back of his skull to drain off what water does get on his brain. Tom, in khaki slacks, a tweed coat, a t-shirt, his hair shiny, sunglasses clipped onto the neckline of his t-shirt, Tom just your regular everyday kind of guy, Tom goes up and squats down beside Leon in his wheelchair, and says, "Leon, my man."

This is when Tom finally grins his famous grin. Leon's a black guy, and like I just said he can barely talk. He shares a room with two people who have to be rotated due to getting bed-sores and fed through g-tubes in their stomachs.

"Hey," Leon says, barely moving his mouth.

Tom whispers, "Hey man."

I stand there, wondering if Tom wants me to stay. I got work to do, people to change, people to feed, people to get baths.

Tom looks up at me, "Gary, is Leon understanding me?"

"I think so."

"Yeah, great," says Tom, smiling at Leon again.

"How's it going bud?"

Leon just sits there.

Tom keeps whispering, "Huh? How's it going? Huh?"

Finally Leon manages, "Good." Slow, almost like he's doing it on purpose.

Tom stands up, looks around the room. I imagine what a movie-star thinks of a retard's bedroom. Probably

how sad it is. Or maybe how fucking inspiring. There's
Leon's poster of Wrestlemania, his dresser with shaving
equipment, his house-slippers cut out in the back because
his feet can devclop sores easy from the scraping of
house-slipper against skin, his poster of Michael Jackson
moonwalking. The walls and ceiling have water-stains
and the smell of shit is still in the air, plus the fried fish or
whatever the cooks have come up with for dinner.

"So what do you do, you and Leon, when you work?"
Tom is asking little old me, as I stand in the doorway.

"Oh, stuff," I say. I try not to make eye contact.

"Stuff," Tom says, laughing.

"Like you know helping him with eating and drinking.
He can't use his arms, so I have to help him eat and drink.
Then maybe we'll get him a bath. Then set him up in the
rec-area to watch TV or sometimes if I get the time we
play Connect-Four. He loves Connect-Four."

Tom nods, serious, like what I just said was the most
profoundest of things. He comes up to me in this serious,
whispery, kind-of fake way, "Hey, what you do is so
important, Gary."

Then again he seems to be for real. Like it's just really
really unfair he makes fifty billion a year and is here with
me, this almost middle-aged queer with his one ear-ring
and frosted hair who pulls down 7.40 an hour wiping
asses.

Like oh well.

Dustin Hoffman comes by as we go toward the kitchen.
Judy, the oldest woman we got here, Judy with chapped

lips and a rat's nest for hair, in a yellow Winnie the Pooh nightgown, is holding Dustin's hand, pulling him in the other direction.

"I think I'm in love," Dustin jokes. The man has a long-assed nose, which I've noticed in movies, but in person it's like a goddamn banana. Some of the people with him laugh, standing at the nurse's station, in the hall, those sunny, serious, California people. One older guy with a sweater and long silver hair and glasses walks up to us.

"Time to go Tom," this guy whispers.

"Hey, Bare, just one look at the kitchen," Tom says.

"Why the kitchen Tom?" Bare asks. "What can you possibly gain from seeing the kitchen?"

"I don't know." Tom laughs, all teeth showing.

A big black lady named Faye is cooking chicken nuggets, not fish, in the deep fryers we have in back. She looks up and smiles.

"Why lookie here," she says.

Tom keeps laughing now, nervously, stupidly.

"What's to eat?" he says. It looks like he can't stop himself now, like he wants to go really bad, but the more he wants to go the less he can make himself move, so there's this little boy face on his face now, this uncomfortable -boy-sitting-in-church-having-to-go-pee face.

"Chicken doodles," Faye says. Her big sweaty face goes a little evil. "By the way, I think you all ought to make more G-movies."

Faye shakes the fry baskets, looking straight at him. She
has rolls and rolls of fat on her upper-arms, hair smashed
in a net, gold-painted fingernails.

"Thanks," Tom says. Meaning it.

Outside, behind the building, the sun is going down.
Dustin and the others have already started saying their
goodbyes, talking to local reporters out front, a major
photo-op. But Tom seems to be hiding. He is looking
at the swing-set built specially for wheelchairs, at the
dumpster. A set of stink-trees sways out by the shoulder
of the interstate. Beside the trees is a basketball goal with
a rusted-off bucket, and a view of mile-long stretch of
storage garages. The sky is orange and big and blowing
out.

"This movie's gonna change some people's minds," Tom
says finally. He seems upset.

I don't know what to say. Don't really know what Tom
is talking about: this the-movie-is-gonna-change-people's
-minds bull-shit. Now what?

I look at him, and he looks back at me, saying: "People
like Leon deserve respect."

"Yeah," I say.

"I mean," he goes on. "They deserve respect just for
surviving."

I light a cigarette, and Tom says, "You got another one?"

"Sure," I say. I give him one. I light it for him, and he
smokes like a teenaged boy nervous before his driving
test. Then it hits me: this guy is Tom Cruise. Is this a

motherfucking dream? All of a sudden, I'm feeling all
gushy and dumb and desperate before him, something
I totally promised myself would not happen as soon
as the social-worker told me they had chosen me to
be Tom Cruise's tour-guide. Chose me because I am
quote-unquote "dedicated." Quote-unquote "the best
direct-care we have."

"Leon," I blurt out, not knowing what the hell I'm
saying. "One time I took Leon home with me for his
birthday."

Tom's eyes go large, like go on go on.

"I took him home with me, and I made him some
lasagna and a birthday cake. I live alone, and it was just
me and Leon watching *Romancing the Stone*, and I got him
a digital watch, but I had to fucking open it for him."

This is like when I get kind of crazy. I start laughing.
For a second, I go almost into tears. Tom gets nervous,
backing away from me a little.

"So I put the watch on his wrist, and we watch the
movie, and it is so dumb, but me and him being alone just
made me feel kind of, um, safe. Safe." I stretch that last
word out a little.

A few moments of silence at this point. I'm thinking
what a great big mistake I just made, letting him hear my
Leon story. Like I wanted to impress him with it, like
Tom Cruise would fall in love with me because I took
Leon home with me, and come Oscar time a certain guy
named Gary from Cincinnati, Ohio would be mentioned
in a certain superstar's acceptance speech.

What a dumb-ass thing to think, or even feel. Then I am staring at Tom Cruise, seeing how short and clean and beautiful he is. Like a wax figure.

"Yeah," goes Tom Cruise, to break the silence, putting his half-smoked cigarette out with the toe of his shoe. He yawns. The guy looks a little scared still.

"Time to go."

Tom Cruise shakes my hand, shakes it and shakes it.

"Thank you," he whispers. "I really got some good ideas. Maybe we can get back together sometime and talk about this stuff some more."

I nod, like I believe him.

So anyways, later that night, after Tom Cruise and Dustin Hoffman and their people leave, I'm changing adult-diapers, doing range of motion exercises with people who got CP issues, feeding the residents who can eat, putting the food bags into people with g-tubes, administering meds, joking around with the other staff about my run-in with celebrity. Cracking them jokes. Always cracking them jokes.

Some new girl who won't make it asks me, "Was he nice?" She's got too much make-up on and I just know one of the residents is going to pull that pretty hair of hers out, the way she's wearing it, all teased up.

But I smile, "Was who nice?" You know, being kind of bitchy.

"Tom Cruise," she says, shocked.

"Yes he was. He was a perfect gentleman." Me still smiling, batting my eye-lashes, just whoring it up. And this

poor girl getting freaked because of my fairy-like manner
now. Other people I work with are laughing of course.
People here are used to my personality. Finally the girl
starts laughing too. Well good for her.

"He's no wham-bam-thank-you-ma'am," I say in my
girliest voice. "He takes it slooooow honey."

This cracks the whole place up.

Then I am alone a little while later, and I get to Leon's
room. It's dark in here, and his roommates are both still
quiet and sleeping. I put him in his bed, adjust the rails.
Leon looks up at me like my own child, I don't have kids
obviously, don't fucking need any, but there he is looking
up at me like he needs something but I don't know what. I
tell him without moving my mouth how sorry I am.

"Sorry for what?" Leon seems to be asking, even though
his lips don't move either.

"Hell, I don't know," I say.

And then I kiss Leon's forehead, and I stand up, and for a
second there we are. Whatever the hell we are. Us.

Of course this was the one and the only time my and
Tom Cruise's paths were ever to cross. One time, though, I
was gonna send him a postcard, as a joke: "We are still here,
Tommy. Come back and see us anytime you can. Loved
the movie. We miss you something awful. Love, Leon and
Gary."

I figured, the man gets millions of fan-letters. What
would be the point?

Gay Day

I had just got off the phone with my mom who was babysitting and bitching, two things she does incredibly well, when all of a sudden Randy came running up and goes, "Somebody got electrocuted. I mean bad."

I was on a smoke-break from my ticket-taking job. It was Gay Day at King's Point, the biggest amusement park in Ohio. I had been working here a couple years, thinking that maybe working at an amusement park might get me closer to show business hell I don't know. Gay Day was fine with me. All the gay people in the tri-state area were here, trying to have fun. They shut the whole park off just for the gay people and they had some Day Glo gay-pride signs up front, and I felt kind of out of my element but still it was something different.

I did not want anybody to get electrocuted. I'm not like that.

Randy's face was red and sweaty and serious, "The log-ride. Somebody fell off a platform waiting to get on and went right into the water and they made contact with the wiring or something. The ambulance is on its way. I swear, it's awful."

He looked like he might cry. Randy is gay and he liked telling us all about it all the time and how Gay Day was the best thing for his community.

"Oh my gosh Randy, I'm sorry."

He bummed a cigarette from me. He wasn't some big manager here. He just picked up garbage and ran rides sometimes, like any other Joe Schmoe, but he had an air about him like he was better than he truly was. He had the dyed blonde hair of someone searching for him or herself. He wore sandals with socks and suspenders over his turquoise T-shirt uniform, with buttons all over it, a leftover I think from his TGIFriday's waitering days. He had to quit there because there was too much cocaine floating around he said.

Randy smoked and I went right on to cigarette number two, and I wondered if we should do something, but since King's Point was so huge, I don't think it mattered. People were still coming into the park. From our point of view, you couldn't see anything but the big water fountain and the Tiptoe the Dragon statue and the huge replica of the Leaning Tower of Pizza.

"How'd you find out?"

"Millie told me."

"Did you see anything?"

"No. But Millie said the body was floating with its face up in the water and blood coming out the eyes."

Randy smoked real hard, and despite the shock of tragedy I kept hearing my mom's low-pitched voice on the phone telling me my little girl had fallen down and busted her head on the coffee-table but it was okay and I told Mom she could have a concussion but Mom put her on the phone.

I asked, "You feel okay sweetie?"

"Mom?"

"What baby?"

"I got a sore place," she said. She did not sound right, like a little toy about to run out its batteries.

"I know. Make Mamaw kiss and make it better."

"Okay."

Mom got back on the phone, "Your little hellion son laughed when she hit her head. I think he's gonna be a gee-dee serial killer. It's like that boy in Florida who was pretending to wrestle and ended up killing his cousin."

"Please Mom just shut up. Quit picking on Brandon."

"Baby the boy and treat the little girl like she's nothing..."

"Yeah that's right Mom. I'm going," I told her.

Now Randy put his cigarette out, all wide-eyed and waiting for the rest of the world to come to an end.

"Gay Day just does not need this kind of publicity," he said, like he had anything to do with publicity for this place.

But I tried to be thoughtful and giving. "Yeah," I said. One time Randy told me he had a friend at TGIFriday's who had done it with Richard Gere, and I just acted like I believed it. It's just easier that way.

"I better go back and see what I can do," he said.

"Was it a man or a woman?"

"A big lady," he says.

"Oh gosh," I say.

"This place is gonna shut down, Adele. They've already got a big lawsuit pending because of what happened on the Dementia."

"I know. It's the way they do things. Profit first."

We heard ambulances then. They were coming in the back way, behind the log-ride.

"I better go."

Randy raced off, and I went back up to ticket booth # 23. It was hot as hell, the sky a bad milk color, and people were still paying to get in, not knowing about the electrocution. I felt a little sorry for all the gay people. I got buzzed back in and I looked out the plexiglass between me and someone else, setting up my cash-drawer, and I saw this sad looking older man with big delicate eyelashes and Richard-Nixon jowls and he had another man with him in a wheelchair, with that same kind of face. They were dressed alike in glittery Hawaiian shirts, and the man standing by the wheelchair said, "Two tickets please."

They both looked pretty happy to be here, despite everything else. For a second I wished I was, you know, a part of it. I'm always envious when people get to do fun things and I have to watch, I guess. I mean, I never had gone over to the other side, except that one time with this gal when I was working at the convenience store, before Michelle was born. She invited me over to her apartment and got me drunk on Jack and Cokes and then she started to kiss me playing Rolling Stones on her CD machine, and I started to laugh real loud knowing what was about to happen and pissed at my ex-boyfriend anyway and then I went ahead and let her do other stuff because she seemed like she wanted to so bad. She looked sort of like Stevie Nix, only fatter with shorter hair.

Anyway, both the old men seemed thrilled but tired, kind of representing the whole human race right then for me. I gave them their tickets by punching them through, and the man said through the plexiglass, "Ohio is not known for its tolerance."

He was talking to me like it would be kept confidential.

"I know," I said. "Have a good time."

He walked his identical friend in the wheelchair through the front gates, past Tiptoe the Dragon, past the Leaning Tower of Pizzas, past the fake hot-air balloons and on into the park itself. I wondered then about the electrocuted lesbian. All she had wanted was to have a good time. For a second, right before I rang through another customer, I wanted to tell them all to vacate the goddamn premises, to run for their lives, to find a place to have fun where people did not die all the time.

Mom said, "Did you see the body?"

"No, I'm up front in the ticket booth, Mom, you know that. King's Point is a huge place."

I had Michelle on my lap, looking at her sore place. It's not very big, but I got this nagging feeling I should take her to the e. r., kind of because it happened on Mom's watch and kind of because it looked real deep.

"I cleaned it with peroxide. I gave her ice-cream. She's okay," Mom said.

"I know. But it looks deep Mom."

This was the trailer we're sharing, not that bad. I know what people say about trailers and I know if I had my choice I would choose an apartment at least, but Mom had bought this double-wide with her retirement money and it was really like a little house. The park we're in is newer, mostly retirees with beautiful lawn furniture and satellite dishes. Mom's richer now after retiring from the plant than she was while working in it. She told me from the get-go that she would babysit but that I had to get my ass a job during the day if we moved in.

Now she had her hair all frosted and puffed out. Her fat friend Judy does it for her, and it looks like a helmet. She has her face made up.

Michelle started to squirm. I let her down. She went to the back of the trailer, kind of wobbly. Brandon was outside somewhere, getting into something I am sure.

"How did it happen? They had it on the news but they didn't say," Mom said.

"I don't know." I just did not feel like going into it. I looked over at the coffee table, at the edge where my daughter's head might have hit and this sent a big chill right through my spine. For some reason on my way home this afternoon I went by the convenience store where I used to work. I went out of my way to do this. I went in and bought myself a pack of cigarettes and the guy who rang me through had brown long hair and a Fu Manchu mustache. He gave me my change and I said, "Does Rhonda still work here?"

"Rhonda who? We got like two Rhondas."

"McCormack?"

"Yeah. She's the manager. She'll be clocking in at six to

work the nightshift because somebody called off and I am not working a double."

"Thanks."

And now Mom said, "Why'd they have a Gay Day anyway?"

"Because they're people too."

Michelle ran into the living room and knocked down Mom's big vase with the goddamn ostrich feathers in it, and then she burst into tears, her eyes looking glassy. Mom went and picked up the huge feathers. I got Michelle, held onto her.

"I'm taking her to the emergency room. She's acting like she's got a concussion. Being cranky is a sign," I said. I felt like I was finally standing up to my mom for like the first time, but Mom just basically ignored me, rearranging the feathers with her big silver head glowing the late light from the mini-blinds.

"Go ahead," she said, not looking up.

"Fine. Watch Brandon. Don't let him get killed."

Mom marched over to me.

"Listen Missy. I can kick you and your kids out of here, you got that? You better stop acting like Miss Big Shot."

Michelle started crying and I knew she had a concussion I knew it deep where Good Mothers know shit like that, that psychic place. Mom just rolled her eyes, feeling the puffiness of her own stupid hair.

"I'm going."

"Go."

Outside I put Michelle in the car-seat and it was not

quite sinking in how my daughter's head might be filling up blood. How my own mom ignored my daughter's brain so she could have some fat lady come over to her trailer and fix her hair. As soon as I saw Michelle in the rearview mirror, I started to cry though. Brandon got in the car then, wet from a hose.

"No. Get in there with Mamaw. I gotta take Michelle to the doctor."

"I wanna go."

I wanted to hit him, but I refrained. I wanted to hug him hard too. He looked like his daddy so much it hurt — and I flashed on that guy, Mark, who I was with back when I thought there might be a future. Mark with his Greenbay Packers jacket he let me wear, and his big-screen TV and his Camaro that got repossessed, and when I told him I was pregnant he said, "That is what we are on this earth for. To procreate." And then two months after Brandon came out he started crying all the time and he said he was bipolar and he had to get some help but then he just disappeared.

"Go on," I said. "I got to take your sister to the doctor now."

Brandon grunted but then got out, running toward the screen door where Mom was standing, smoking a cigarette, a small-boned woman with wrinkled brown skin and that hair. She looked like a crow in the eye department. But she loved Brandon you could tell.

I didn't even wave goodbye to them.

They took an x-ray, but there was nothing wrong. I
made sure they showed me the X-ray because I am that
kind of mother. I have a picture I cut out of a nature
magazine of a mother lioness looking fierce as hell. It's
Scotch-taped to my bathroom mirror.Michelle was fine
through the whole e. r. ordeal. She had to have two
stitches, which I was going to make sure Mom heard
about. On the way back I took the long route home.
Michelle was groggy from the pain medicine they gave
her, and she fell to sleep in the car seat back there, and I
somehow managed to park in the Village Pantry parking
lot. It was still muggy out, and there were people inside
the store, waiting in line. I sat in my car and I thought
about how I used to pull up here to work, and how after
that one night when Rhonda and me did it I felt guilty
how Rhonda came to the store all dressed up and she
gave me an old-fashioned bouquet of flowers. It was
more than weird and I thought about beating her up.

I remembered standing inside that store at the register
and it was like midnight. Rhonda pulled up in her old
car and she had on a pants outfit and her hair was parted
in the middle, perfectly hairsprayed and she even had
on makeup which looked kind of stupid on her really.
Too much, too glossy. She had that big bouquet and she
looked like she was lost.

She stepped into the store and she said, "Surprise."

"Hi," I said, thinking about what we did and how I did
not ever want to do it again but then there was something
else too, how easy it was to do it, and how real it got

when she was happy to do it to me. How I just laid back and she went to town on me, and I thought about having sex with the guys I have had sex with and how it was never like that, how they never really seemed to enjoy it, they just wanted to have it over with except when they were fucked up, and even then it was like a big show they were putting on, especially Mark, the deadbeat dad of my kids.

Rhonda looked hurt when she saw my expression.

"I thought you got off at midnight," she said.

"No. I'm doing a double."

"Oh. I thought we might go to Denny's."

"Sorry."

"That's okay."

Then she stood there, and I put the flowers on the back table. We could not talk. I was sorry for her predicament, mine too, but then again I wanted her to know that what I did with her was a one-time-only deal. But she kept looking at me like I was the only one in the world and I smiled back at her, pissed yet somehow flattered.

"You're beautiful," she whispered.

Then there was a customer coming in, and another. Rhonda stood beside me, gabbing. I wanted her to go. But all she did was stand there till three in the morning. We talked about nothing bull-shit, and finally when she was about to go she said, "I love you."

And I said, "Come on. Cut it out."

She said, "Really. I am in love with you."

"Well sorry hon. No way. Last night was it."

She tried to laugh it off like a joke, "Right."

"I mean it Rhonda. I'm not a dyke."

"I know. That's why it's so perfect."

"Shut up."

I was tired okay, and I wanted to go home so bad, and then I said real mean, "It kind of makes me sick you being here."

Rhonda just laughed. I saw her lose something though in the laugh, like a part of what she thought she had gripped tight and solid in her hand was just melted ice-cream, sticky and warm. She came over to me and got into my space and she tried to kiss me, and I told her to get the fuck away and that's when I hit her pretty hard, and she reeled back and fell onto the floor.

Somebody came in and then walked back out, scared. Then I head Muzak still going. It was almost funny that way she tried to get up and fell down again, funny in a real bad way, and the next day she left seven messages on my machine and I felt like I was being harassed so I just did not go back into work. I just quit without telling anybody.

I changed my phone number. I got myself another job.

Now I was back here at the Village Pantry, and I was getting out of the car. I was wondering if it might have been her who got electrocuted. I was wondering I think if maybe there could be such a coincidence in the world, and also how I broke somebody's heart that night the way mine was so often broken. That night I knocked Rhonda down, I'd felt the power of being someone's loved one

and I felt the urge to run from her, the way guys have
ran from me. It wasn't like revenge. It was more like a
reaction animals might have to dig tunnels or to fly into
windows.

Rhonda spotted me right off, after the person in line
in front of me got his cigarettes. She turned around and
saw me. She had gained weight since two years ago. She
looked miserable and scared and then kind of happy to see
me.

"Well lookie here," she said.

I glanced out the window real quick, to make sure
Michelle was okay. She was still asleep with the big Band-
aid on her forehead, her mouth all the way open.

Rhonda had cut her hair so short it was like an Army
buzz, and she didn't have any makeup on. She looked
kind of handsome in a way.

"Yeah, it's me."

Rhonda opened the cash register and took out some
bills and counted them.

"Where you been?"

"I'm living with my mom."

"That's good."

She stopped looking at me, and then looked out at my
old car.

"That your baby?"

"Yeah."

I knew this was a huge and stupid mistake and I did not
know why I was even here but I felt compelled somehow
to let her know she was okay.

"I work at King's Point," I told her.

"Somebody got killed out there today, didn't they? Electrocuted?" She still was not looking at me. She was putting the bills back. She was slamming the cash drawer. She grabbed a rag and wiped off the deli counter.

"Yeah," I said.

The smell of the store brought back the memory of what she'd done to me, coolers and bleach and meat. I think I really did love her back then. She did not really disgust me as much as scare me, and I wanted her to know that there once was a time when I felt like I almost could go there but then there was always that feeling like no man would have me and so I would have to turn lesbo. That hurt like a burn. It was my pride, and I kept thinking of how my mom called my kids' dad a gee-dee bum and they heard that, they had to, and there their mom would be: the big stupid dyke.

Rhonda stopped wiping the counter off.

"Why don't you just leave?" She was crying, I noticed, and I thought about going behind that counter and kissing her on the mouth, the sporadic lioness thing to do, to let her know I was sorry and maybe to tell her we could try it again. I wanted someone, anyone, right then. I wanted to be able to call home and not get Mom.

"Go on," she said.

"I'm sorry," I said.

I went back out to the car and I pulled out real quick, shaking a little, and I looked back and there was Michelle, still sleeping, her head all bandaged up.

Brandon and Michelle shared a room in the back of Mom's trailer. He had his race-car bed. Michelle was in a small twin with a pink comforter Mom bought. Mom was out in the living room watching *Dateline*.

"She had a slight concussion," I told Mom as soon as I got Michelle into bed. When I had first come in, she kept asking and I just ignored, carrying Michelle into the house like she was a victim of war-torn Bosnia. I got a beer and I drank half of it.

"She did not."

Mom was pissed.

"Yes she did. And she got stitches. Stitches, Mom. Okay?" My voice was a little intense.

"She did not," she said in a whisper.

"Mom I'm not lying!"

"Bull. She was fine."

"Fuck it," I said.

We watched the TV show she wanted to watch. Then Mom got up silently and went to her over-decorated bedroom. I pulled the bed out of the couch and watched whatever else was on. Then I turned the TV off and it got real quiet. I kept seeing Rhonda's face and how she had gained so much weight and how she was crying and how she got management at the store. I plotted our lives out together for us. She would be a good mother, I thought. But I knew I was just being desperate.

I got up then, like a sleepwalker. I got up like I sometimes do and quietly, like a prowler, went into the

kids' room. I crawled into bed with my son and held
him and he stirred. He smelled like cereal. I looked
over at Michelle. She was asleep, the bandage glowing
in the moonlight, and I thought about how maybe next
weekend I could take them to King's Point because my
family-members can get in free, they'd like that, I think,
and I would make sure nothing happened to them there,
and I knew this is what I would have to end up with,
these two, me and them, and then I got to the point
where I could finally go to sleep.

Dark Eyes

1

Mr. Dawson, the owner, called every night around ten, his voice raspy and low. I was the night manager of his restaurant.

"Bring me some of those breaded mushrooms, will you, Markus?" Mr. Dawson said, this one particular night. He was home-bound and dying of something. Nobody knew exactly what.

"Anything else?" I was smiling. The electronic buzzer on the drive-thru went off. Katrina, the girl who was working, and my fiancee's best friend, went over to get it but knocked down a tray of empty pie pans. It made a huge racket.

"What's going on?" Mr. Dawson asked.

"Oh nothing."

"Sounded like the end of the world."

"Just a little accident."

The speaker let out a big goat-like growl, as a man outside in his car was telling Katrina he wanted a large chili and a Big-D burger. He had a deep-pitched sissy-type voice.

"So do you want anything else tonight?" I asked.

"Could you stop off and get me a bottle of Dark Eyes?" Mr. Dawson asked.

"Dark Eyes?" I asked.

"Yeah. Dark Eyes vodka."

He laughed again, embarrassed. This was the first time
he had ever requested anything like that. He used to sing
gospel, I was thinking, and on the juke box out in the
dining room were all his family's albums, and when kids
played the juke-box it was Back Street Boys, that kind of
stuff, but then sometimes by accident they would press the
wrong button and suddenly The Dawson Family Singers
were singing "How Great Thou Art."

"Sure," I said.

"Take the money out of tonight's deposit."

He hung up. I looked out the drive-thru window.
Katrina had it open, and cold air was blowing in. An
elegant old man with silver styled hair was sitting in his
cream-colored luxury car. I wondered what a class act
like that was doing coming here to this place. This was
a rundown burger joint, when you get right down to it.
Big-D Family Restaurant.

I smiled at the elderly gentleman, but he stuck a
cigarette in his mouth and lit it with the car lighter. He
was talking secretively to someone else beside him in the
car, but I could not make out that person through the
window.

Katrina bagged the old man's order. I went over and
started picking up the pie pans, and soon as I stood
up with them all, I looked out the drive-thru window
again. This time, I saw the guy in the seat next to the old
man. He was leaning forward laughing. A young man,
with dark eyelashes and big eyes. I tried not to look too
long. His hair was very black, as though it were dyed,

and he looked muscular even in the shadows of passing
headlights. He winked at me. I knew he was only having
fun with me. I'm an obese guy. Lets get it out on the
table. Obese and going bald and about to be married to
an obese woman who loves me very much.

I winked back though.

The guy in the passenger seat started to laugh his
head off. The old man took the bag from Katrina and
practically threw it at the young man. He pulled away.

Katrina, skinny with a thick mountain accent and
orange hair, turned around, "God, what a couple of fags."

Rod, Katrina's husband, usually comes inside to wait for
her to finish. He is a young guy who likes to hunt and
that's about it, outside of petty theft and roofing. Tonight
he was out in the maroon booth in front, waiting. I
joined him to finish my paperwork as Katrina washed the
final dishes. The paneling out here was warped, and the
beige cork ceiling tiles had big stains on them from leaks.
Portraits of Jesus Christ in different styles were hung up
above the booths. Rod was over putting a quarter into
the jukebox. He chose a hard rock song.

"Monique said you were going to elope," he said,
turning around.

"Yep, probably. We're both just sick of all the wedding
crap," I said, penciling in inventory sheets. I'd known
Rod since high school, but we weren't real friends till
Monique, that's my fiancee, and me started dating back
five years ago.

"Me and Katrina eloped," Rod said now, shuffling back to slouch in a booth.

"I know, Monique and I already live together, so it's like some sacred ritual we're just too damn tired to do."

Rod played with the salt-and-pepper shakers like action figures. He was a little kid that way, hyper with wild hair and small eyes, but he has a pretty face. Katrina came out and plopped down beside me.

"You tell him about those two fags that came through?" she said, pulling her cigarettes out of her purse.

"No," I said, still filling in numbers. Mr. Dawson always double-checked.

"Goddam," Katrina said, pulling her apron off. She was very skinny.

"What?" Rod looked up with wide eyes.

"This old prissy faggot and his boy-toy come through drive-through. It was gross."

Katrina laughed, dragged off her cigarette. Rod pushed the shakers back toward the wall and made bongo sounds on the table, looking a little pissed, "What the hell were they doing coming out here?"

"I do not know," Katrina said, blowing out smoke.

I slumped my shoulders. I looked at Rod and saw him naked that morning before he blew the head off a groundhog. This was from one time when he and I had gone on a hunting trip. He was in the bathroom of the state park cabin we had rented, with the door wide open. Peeing in the nude. I felt protected being on a hunting trip, so I could look. As he peed, he sang something. For a second, it was almost beautiful.

I thought of Mr. Dawson wanting Dark Eyes vodka then. Thought of telling Katrina and Rod about him ordering the vodka. Like I was telling on him. But they were leaving now anyway.

"I think I might do some mushrooms," Rod said.

"You doing mushrooms? On a week night? Well, don't you mess up my house," Katrina said. She hit at him playfully.

"Woman," Rod said, making fists in kidding way. That's what he called her. "Woman, watch yourself." He looked at me like he wanted me to back him up.

"I left the fryer on so you could do the holy roller's midnight snack," Katrina said, rolling her eyes. She did not like Mr. Dawson that much. He used to get on her for smoking and stuff. "Tell him we're praying for him." She looked like she meant that though.

"Thanks. See you guys later."

I went and dropped the breaded mushrooms into the black grease, and the breading foamed up orange. As they fried, I called Monique.

"I gotta run by Mr. Dawson's," I said.

Her voice was excited. "I made some coffee, and now I'm buzzing. I got an anatomy test tomorrow." She was studying to be an LPN at East Tennessee Vocational.

"Yeah, well, I'll see you when I get home."

"You okay?" The sweetness in her voice sometimes made my muscles hurt. This was an ugly feeling because I truly loved her. I thought of us having sex. It was not

something people want to read about in a book I know.
Two 300 pounders going at it, but we did it in a nice
polite style. Careful, with the lights off, under the covers,
losing ourselves in it, losing what we thought of ourselves.
That's where we helped each other out a lot. Plus we
didn't get on each other about eating.

"I'm fine," I said.

"Okay honey."

I hung up, and went over to see the mushrooms. They
were floating like little severed heads in a hot black lake.

The mountains in October are very pretty, even this
time at night. The leaves give off a glow like backward
light, an X ray of bones done in burgundy and silver. Mr.
Dawson lived out in a holler where they are building new
houses all over the place, but his, a long ranch-style they
built with their gospel money, was older and had a big
tall fence presumably to keep their fans away. Missy, Mr.
Dawson's daughter, had her own show on the Christian
cable network. Terry, the son, died ten years ago in a
motorcycle wreck. Mrs. Dawson died back in the early
eighties from unchecked breast cancer I think it was.

I'd gotten the Dark Eyes vodka at a liquor store on the
way, and now it rolled on the car floor as I pulled into Mr.
Dawson's. His was a white-brick house, with mint-green
trim and rococo shutters made out of wrought-iron. A
big bird bath sat in front of the front stoop, and there was
an abandoned rock garden. The gate was already open.

Mr. Dawson opened the door before I got there. Tall

with his wig on, his jowls hanging down his face, he had on a dark robe with slippers and pajamas. His wig was dark brown and curly, like his hair used to be, and he had a real thin mustache above his lip. Behind him I heard the Dawson Family Singers singing on a tape or album. I don't think any of their music ever made it to CDs.

"Hello," he said.

I nodded and gave him the tally sheets, vodka, and breaded mushrooms, like this was my offering. Usually what would happen was he would take them and talk to me about that night's business and then I would go. But on this particular night he seemed scared.

"So how did it go?" he asked. His smile was tight, as if he were stretching it against extreme pain.

"Pretty good. We had some stuff after the basketball game over in Hampton. Lots of drive-thru action."

A wind blew, dragging dead leaves across the ground.

"Why don't you come in?" Mr. Dawson asked me.

"Okay," I said.

The inside of his house I'd seen only once before, when he told me to come over to pick him up because his car was in the shop. I remembered seeing the house then in June sunshine, dusty, glassy and ornate. All that ornateness now seemed to have been dredged up from underwater, like the Titanic. There was that singing too. Deep-pitched males and soft-pitched females, harmonizing about Jesus in the garden alone. Organ and piano keys tinkling and humming. It was too loud.

Mr. Dawson turned on the chandelier. We walked

down into the sunken den. As soon as the lights were on, he went over to his bar with the black-vinyl stools around it. He opened the Dark Eyes and poured a lot into a tumbler.

I knew he must have been in a lot of pain. He could barely tilt his head back to drink the stuff. "I used to go out and get it myself. But I can't any more. Hurts too much to go out." He kind of laughed. "Cold air on my skin."

The walls were covered in pictures from their gospel days. I looked, like I was in a museum. They were all healthy in 1973, Missy in a polyester skirt and lavender frilly blouse, her hair teased high, like her mom's, and the men were in lavender leisure suits, Terry with his hair cut military-short, but his dad's was curly and full. One picture showed them on a stage with microphones on stands, in the middle of a concert, frozen in time.

Mr. Dawson drank about three tumblers full. No kidding. It was like he was showing off. After that, he took a deep, deep breath.

By then the album was done. He walked over, stumbling, and pulled the needle off. His stereo equipment was expensive and impressive, lots of shiny gadgetry. The needle scratched across the record, and he laughed a belly laugh, then put on another album.

"Softly and Tenderly" came on. Mr. Dawson started to sing along. In that moment, he seemed perfectly fine. He was happy to be drunk and singing. Despite everything, I was not thinking of Mr. Dawson right then. I was thinking about something I did long ago. When I was 12 or 13, before my older cousin went into the Army. He and I were in the garage of his house beside the riding lawn mower, hiding back there, and on the floor of the garage while we did what we did I saw a Christmas ornament that had fallen from a box, a red bulb that had smashed into a thousand little egg-shell-like pieces. The music was making me go back because my cousin and I would often go to church together. I remembered as soon as my cousin told me to get my underwear back on, I remembered wanting to eat the broken ornament like candy.

Then Mr. Dawson fell down onto the floor. I heard something crack.

"Are you all right?" I said, going over.

He fell back, still singing, but it was almost like he was asleep. My knees hurt as I squatted down. He reached up. His hands were shaking, and the music made me feel woozy, and I smelled the vodka on him.

"I want you to pray with me, Markus."

I nodded. The music was "The Old Rugged Cross." I heard the family harmonizing. I heard the organs.

"Dear Jesus," he said. He gripped my hand as tight as possible. "Let me go. Jesus. Let me go. I'm tired of this. I'm tired of it. I'm tired."

I sat down on the floor beside him, and it hit me that I should call an ambulance, but I stayed in this moment, in the half lit cave-like room with pictures from 1973.

I knew I should get up, but then as soon as I tried Mr.

Dawson looked up at me, and he said, "Don't."

This is when he grabbed onto me and he kissed me. He had to kiss somebody right then, I guess.

Then he sat up, on the floor. His eyes were wide open. He looked at me and smiled.

"I think you better leave," he said, clear as day. He coughed real deep.

"You want me to call an ambulance or doctor or something?"

"No," he said. "No. I'm just fine."

He got up very slowly, in pain still, but exhausted. He walked over to the big couch and laid down on it. He laid back like he was practicing for his casket. Mr. Dawson opened his eyes.

"Thank you for being such a good employee," he said.

I didn't even see Rod's car out in front of our apartment, so when I went in I was a little shocked that he and Katrina were there. All three of them were having pizza. Monique took up most of the couch, but Katrina was next to her. It was funny, of course. Big fat woman and skinny little woman. Rod was over by the breakfast bar, shaking like he was having a seizure.

"Hey you guys," I said.

Monique had just got her hair permed, and it was like a tight brown helmet. It made her face look lost, like the eyes were being pulled back by the inside of her hair. She had on a housecoat. Katrina was in sweats, and Rod didn't have his shirt on.

"I am hot!" he said, shaking still.

Katrina laughed. "He did those damn mushrooms, Markus. I swear to God. I bet they were poison. Where'd you get them?"

Rod stepped over. He stood in front of me. His flesh was dark even in the fall. He spent all summer doing roofs.

"Some old boy at the vocational school sells them. Hey, Markus, you wanna try some?"

Rod turned around and dangled the bag in front of me. I looked at the mushrooms inside. They were black and stringy, like shoelaces.

I looked at Monique, and she was eating a big slice, the cheese hanging off. I thought about how the other night we'd planned our honeymoon. We were going to go to Gatlinburg and stay in a condo in the mountains and go shopping for antique furniture. We were going to buy a house as soon as she got her LPN license. Actually, we were looking forward more to the honeymoon than anything else, because her mom, who was kind of rich, was giving us 2000 dollars to buy the furniture with.

I took a mushroom from Ricky. I saw his nipples. He had gobs of hair under his arms. One time when there was this kid who got killed in Knoxville for being a homosexual and it was on the news, Rod got up and quoted the Bible, or at least the Bible according to Rod. He said, "Thou shalt not suffer a faggot to live." He was very serious. "It's in the Bible," he kept saying all that night until all of us said okay.

I swallowed the mushroom whole.

Monique turned on the TV, and I relaxed on a lounger. Rod was wired though.

"I think I'm seeing visions," he said, leaning back on the bar, showing off. His face was an actor's face, but not a good actor.

Katrina said, "Oh please shut up."

"No. Really."

His eyes widened. "Big fucking animals, man. Without their skins on. Coming out the walls."

Katrina turned to Monique, "He makes this crap up."

Monique just nodded, eating, quiet.

"Fucking skinless coons man," Rod said, laughing, eyes wide as flashlights, on his knees now like a rock star. He slammed into the couch next to Katrina, saying, "Protect me, Woman. Those fuckers are gonna eat me alive!"

Monique wanted to hold my hand, standing beside the chair now, but I got up and laughed. She gave me a dirty look. "I wish you wouldn't take drugs, Markus," she half-whispered.

Katrina said, "They are just boys, that's all. Boys will be boys." She was patting Rod's small head on the sofa.

Rod looked up. He was scared, you could tell.

"I think I'm gonna puke," he said.

I got up then, took his hand in mine. Right when I did that, I allowed myself to pretend I was stoned. Or maybe I was. Still when I took his hand, the roughness of his fingers seemed to dig into more than my palm — more like they were digging up the dirt inside my skull. He had a blank sick-baby face.

"I am gonna puke," he said again.

Katrina laughed, but looked worried. "I told you, Rod. I told you."

For a moment, I got my composure. "I'll take him into our bathroom."

Katrina said, "You are so nice, Markus."

But Monique was not looking at me now. She was going for the pizza.

I pushed Rod into the bathroom and shut the door behind us, locking it. All of Monique's skin stuff was spread out on the sink, like medications. She pampered herself that way.

"Man," Rod said, landing on his knees in front of the commode. "There was something bad wrong about them shrooms."

I started to shiver a little, and I felt the hungry jaws of my feelings opening and spilling out a secret drug.

Rod could not puke, so he sat back against the wall, and I turned the lights out.

"Hey," he said, but it got quiet as I stood there. I knocked over a bottle of lotion, and it whirled in the sink.

I stooped down to my knees. My eyes adjusted to the dark in here. Then I saw Rod's eyes. They were glowing slightly from the light that was sneaking in under the crack under the door. He looked shocked and ill, but then I could hear something like coins falling out of pockets.

"Man, I am so fucked up," he whispered. He started

laughing, and I reached down to him, half of my shoulder on the top of the commode lid, and then I heard his belt buckle hit the floor and I heard the zipper, and my hand reached down to him. I felt it. I remembered all the other times I used to do it with my cousin, all the other times I had wanted to do it. How blood rushed and roared, how one moment sparkled out like a terrorist bomb as quiet as toes inside socks squirming from some real good pleasure.

As I started playing with it, I heard Rod moan and whimper: "I am so fucked up. God. Damn. Fucked. Up."

I stopped and leaned down, breathing hard and then I somehow took it into my mouth. I thought of the way fish might do it underwater and that made me get harder. Thought of little dumb animals underground. What they must do to each other because of nature. I wanted Rod to shut up.

"Those fucking shrooms man."

Right when his stuff shot out, I saw Mr. Dawson in my head, an old man asleep in a grand house in the woods. The sleep of the dead in that house, and his peacefulness spread into me like phone-talk through wires, like the voice he used when he called me asking me to bring him vodka, bring him food, bring him something that will make him want to stay alive.

I pulled my mouth off Rod's thing, sat back against the wall in the dark.

There was a knock on the door.

"You guys okay?" It was Katrina.

Rod pulled his pants up quick. He stood up and got the lights, and I saw him glance at me in the light. I had pulled my own thing out. With the lights on, I spurted out stuff all over myself. He looked at the light switch after seeing me, and he yelled, "Man these shrooms are fucked, Katrina." He made sure the door was locked. "We'll be out in a second."

Rod and Katrina left real quick after we came out of the bathroom. Monique started studying again. I sat down on the chair and imagined the furniture we were going to buy on our honeymoon. I wondered about kids. Her doctor told her she would have to lose 150 pounds to get pregnant. So we might adopt.

"I love you," I told her, sitting there.

She glanced up from her big heavy anatomy book. "Come here," she said.

I got up and went over to her. She showed me what she was studying. An autopsy of splayed skin, all the muscle groups pulled back with brackets. A real dead body.

"This is so interesting," she whispered. She kept staring at the book. I heard some hurt in her voice, but I ignored it. I just wanted us to go on, and I knew we would, and once we got older, once we got into a total routine we would know how to proceed without thinking. The part that messes things up would be cut out by the invisible scissors known as time.

"I have to know every muscle," she told me, truly serious.

2

"I need two bottles, Markus," Mr. Dawson spoke the next night.

"Two bottles?" I asked.

"Dark Eyes," he said, and he hung up.

Katrina was counting ones. "Wonder if those fags are gonna come back?" she asked. She kind of smiled.

"Probably not," I said.

She laughed really loud, but I laughed too.

"Man, Rod was so sick last night. Mushrooms are bad to take. Just smoke you some dope, I keep telling him." Katrina nervously slid the bundles of dollar bills back into the drawer and slammed it shut.

At the end of closing, Rod did not pick her up, so I walked her out to her car.

"He's still feeling pretty bad. He had to take off work," Katrina told me as she lit up a cigarette before getting into her car.

"Wow," I said. "I feel okay."

"Yeah," she said. She got into her car, and then rolled the window down. "Didn't Mr. Dawson want something to eat?"

"No, he just called about how business went," I said. I didn't want to tell her that I was fueling his alcohol habit, of course.

She pulled away. I knew we would all be friends for a very long time, me and Monique and Rod and Katrina, because this was a small town, and in small towns the people you grow up with are the only people you can really count on.

I bought the vodka. Two bottles. I went to Mr. Dawson's house. I knocked on his door, surprised that he was not waiting on me. I started pounding on it. It flung open.

"Mr. Dawson?"

I put the bottles down on the floor, hearing gospel music echoing through the house. I walked on into the sunken den. Mr. Dawson was sprawled on the floor naked, like he had pulled off all his clothes, agitated and tired of being covered up. Blood, red as beets, spilled down his chin and down his neck. He looked like a starfish with a broken head.

I bent down, careful not to get into any blood. He was not alive anymore. His eyes were wide open, like weddings rings missing their diamonds. I automatically went to the phone. Thought about calling an ambulance, but what I wound up doing was calling Rod and Katrina's. Rod answered.

"Hey," I said. I could see just part of Mr. Dawson in his living room.

"What?" Rod asked.

"You mad at me?" I asked.

"No. Just don't feel good."

"I need some help," I said.

"What?"

"Could you come out to Mr. Dawson's house. You know? Near Black Bottom?"

"Why?"

"He's got all this booze," I said.

"Mr. Dawson? Holy Roller?"

"Yeah." I laughed, not knowing what else I could do, and then finally I stopped laughing.

"So?" I said.

"Okay," Rod said.

I hung up and went back out to the den. The music had stopped, and I went and put on another album. This one was The Dawson Family Singers On Calvary. I looked down at Mr. Dawson and thought about the fact that all the people on the record except one were dead, and she really didn't have anything to do with him due to some money and court things. I went and got the vodka bottles and I started drinking from one of them. For some reason, I felt compelled to take the wig off Mr. Dawson's head. I supposed I wanted him to be exactly the way he was in death, not hiding anything, including baldness. His bald head began to stare at me, however, and with the music and the vodka along came God, like a mushroom high, and I saw what seemed like a mist rise out of the blood coming out of Mr. Dawson's mouth. I wondered to myself, sitting down on the sofa, if what I was doing was crazy or just completely despicable.

All my whole life I could hide everything away, let it

stay and turn to ice inside me and then melt it down at night, and then I would suck it back up as liquid, not ice: melted feelings tasting like melted food, watery and flavorless.

Then Rod came in, as I had left the front door wide open.

"Jesus Fucking Christ," he said, looking around the room, going over to Mr. Dawson's body. Rod was in an army coat and blue jeans and black t-shirt, hiking boots, his curly hair oily and sleep-shaped. He looked like he had just gotten out of jail.

"What the hell?" Rod said.

I got up and offered him my bottle of vodka. He looked at me like I was insane. I took a drink, and realized this is what Mr. Dawson had drank to kill the pain, the actual pain that had made the blood explode.

"This guy is fucking dead," Rod said.

"I know."

"Did you kill him?" Rod kind of laughed then.

"No. He was this way when I found him. I swear to God."

Rod went and turned the music off.

"Jesus," he said.

It got real quiet.

"Did you call an ambulance?" Rod asked.

"No," I said. "Not yet."

I walked to Rod then, past Mr. Dawson. He was scared of me, I felt that, and I took his hand in mine.

"Come here," I said.

He let me take his hand because he was afraid. The whole house was empty, except for the owner's body. I led Rod down the hall from the living room past a lavender bedroom and then into a smaller one at the back. I turned on the lights. It was a boy's bedroom, with motorcycle posters on the wall, and a small twin-bed with plaid spread on it. A desk with a sail-boat lamp and a Holy Bible on it, like a museum set-up. This was where Mr. Dawson's son used to sleep when he was alive.

Rod stepped in with me, and I pushed him onto the bed, and he started to laugh.

"There's a fucking dead guy out there, Markus," Rod said.

I went to him, and I bent down to him like a grizzly bear, and I kissed his mouth so hard he cried out.

"Fucker," he said, looking up at me, breathing hard. I could tell he wanted to punch me, so I grabbed his arms. I kissed him again, and I started to tear his clothes off. He allowed me. I bit into him at times, tasting his flesh, and it was gasoline-sweet, a dark flavor like when meat sets out on the table too long. When I took his thing into my mouth, I felt Mr. Dawson out in the living room, felt the blood-bloom from his mouth blossom into a red color, like sirens bursting on a wall. I wanted nothing else right then: to be alive and Mr. Dawson be dead because when he was dead, I was here in his house, doing this.

When we stopped, I left Rod alone, and I walked back out into the hall. Somehow the music had gotten turned back on. I stumbled into the living room, and there he

was, Mr. Dawson, dead and naked, but the needle was
back on the record. It was a song I did not know the
name of, but it had pretty words in it about the blood and
the cross and the lamb. All the pictures on the walls were
singing, I thought.

Suddenly Rod was behind me. He stepped slowly
over Mr. Dawson's body, to the stereo set-up. He snuck
up behind the entertainment center, unplugging the
turntable, unhooking the speakers. He kept quiet all the
way through. I stood and watched as he rolled the cords
up, took the speakers out to his car. He wrapped the
electric wires around the tape-player, took the TV too.

After all that, Rod came back in, coughing and looking
down at the floor.

"Now," he said. "What else you want to take?"

The Smallest People Alive

1

Phyllis made liver and onions the first night I was there, with peas and microwaved hash-browns. Ben, her son and my used-to-be best friend, ate Cinnamon Toast Crunch cereal as an act of defiance.

"Yummy yummy," Phyllis whispered loudly, chewing and smiling, like it was a commercial for the Liver and Onions Council.

Chuck, Ben's dad, just laughed at his end of the table. He had on his greasy Armco cap, his face pale and in need of a shave. Phyllis, by the way, was in a pair of red sweats pulled up to her knees and bare-footed with one of Chuck's old flannel shirts on, her dyed black hair pony-tailed with a rubber-band.

Ben sat above his bowl of cereal, not furious, just resolute. He was skinny, his face drawn-in, the tracheotomy scar glowing pink above the neckline of a faded Hootie and the Blowfish tee. With that, he wore acid-washed jeans and hiking boots with sweat-socks, resting his left arm on the dinette table, the arm that didn't work that well, while he spooned cereal in with the right. His walker, silver aluminum with dirty white tape on the tops for handles, little wheels on its front legs, sat beside the brown refrigerator behind the table like a robot sidekick.

Chuck said, "Good God Phyllis, this is just the best liver,

I mean ever. You out-did yourself." He looked around the
table, then wheezed out his sweet-toned red-neck laugh.

It was obvious this whole dinner-thing they were doing
was a great big put-on, a way of taunting Ben into eating
what they were, and also a way to get rid of some other
feelings without really going into anything serious. After
Chuck laughed, though, it just went quiet again.

Me? I was sitting next to Phyllis, eating what Chuck
and Phyllis were, and I guess I could describe myself as a
22-year-old, not very tan male, on the verge of obesity,
with short, professionally cut hair, done by Adam, the guy
I live with. I was wearing a button-down shirt, jeans a
little too tight because I refuse to go above a 42 waist size.
This tonight, believe it or not, was the start of my vacation
here, in McCordsville, Ohio, with Ben and Phyllis and
Chuck. I had come all the way from Dayton, 60 miles
from the North.

Intermittently I looked at Ben as he ate his cereal,
as I cut up my liver. Looked up and got the feeling
that he knew I was pitying him so he was playing his
part, spooning cereal slowly into his 22-year-old baby
mouth, the milk dripping from the spoon onto the
vinyl tablecloth. Defiant, situated in his chair as if to be
spotlighted.

To break the silence again, Phyllis said, "These hash-
browns...." But then she stopped chewing so elaborately,
stopped smiling. "These hash-browns are not done," she
said to herself, pissed. She got up like she was putting
out a fire, went to the counter and grabbed a spatula and

platter, scooped the hash-browns from Chuck and my
plates. Silent, Phyllis put the platter into her huge, ancient
microwave, turned it on with the dial.

Ben started laughing.

"Shut up," said his mom.

Ben laughed sluggishly, as his speech had been affected,
his voice, his face, his eyes, his everything. It happened
two years ago. It, like the book by Stephen King. It was
pretty simple, though, not enough maybe for a whole
novel of unrelenting terror, but tragic, the way things
out in the country can get. Two years ago, Ben had tried
to off himself in the garage, the one right outside the
kitchen window over there. Ben parked his piece-of-
shit, sky-blue bucket of bolts Plymouth Volare in that
garage, clogged what gaps existed in windows and doors
with cheap caulking, attached a hose to the exhaust pipe
with silver duct-tape, then slipped the hose into the front
seat and sat back to die. Even though he had taken as
many precautions as humanly possible, Ben still survived
obviously. The roof was full of holes. His dad came home
to get lunch and found him and called 911.

Ben looked up when Phyllis told him to shut up,
laughing like that. Then he stopped. He slammed his
spoon into his bowl, milk going everywhere.

"What... What. Did you. Say?" he yelled in his
brain-damaged speak, sentences chopped up into stalled
segments. His face got completely red. It was like he was
going to wish them into the cornfield, like that little kid
in the Twilight Zone episode.

"I told you to shut up that awful laughing," Phyllis said, turning around, this time grinning. The microwave dinged.

Chuck went, "Hey, Ben. Mike's here. Mikie."

I smiled, like my presence meant anything. Ben did not look at me, milk dripping onto the beige linoleum. He continued to sit in his chair, his face puppet-like when a puppet is in a suitcase waiting to be used, the left eye bigger than the right, blinkless and bigger.

Suddenly, he let out a blood-curdling scream. Phyllis brought the hash-browns back. Ben kept howling.

"We just ignore," Phyllis says, her face disgusted. Chuck ate the hash-browns, keeping his head down.

Ben stopped finally. Panting, he stared at me. He looked exhausted, but also you could see in his eyes that he wanted to scream more, scream louder, knowing it would not do anything anyway. Still the desire was there.

I smiled again. My own stupid smile. Milk kept dripping.

"Yes," Phyllis said. "He will clean that up." She was talking to herself.

Of course, Phyllis cleaned it. Ben just got up and got his walker and went into the living room. The walker had been a matter of contention for most of the time I'd been here, since two that afternoon, arriving in my own piece-of-shit bucket of bolts Dodge Colt, me the Vacation Boy having gotten a week off from Winn Packaging, where I took plastic bottles from molding machines 6P-6A four nights a week.

That walker was greeting me on the front porch of their blonde-brick ranch-style. Phyllis had put it out there like a bad dog. I knocked on the screen-door upon arriving. Ben was inside the house, inside the screen, wobbling. He looked at me with sour curiosity.

"Get. That," he ordered.

I had my duffel bag, so I put that down and scooted the walker toward me, opened the door, gave the walker to him.

"Thanks," he said, gripping and fondling the top handles.

I joked, "Nice to see you too."

He raised his eyes slowly and smiled. "Hey," he said.

His mom came in then, same outfit as she would be wearing at dinner: "The physical therapist said he should try going without that." Tense, she walked up, drying her hands on a dish-towel. Then her expression changed to formal all-out happiness. "Welcome Mikie," she said, looking at the walker with disgust. "We are glad to have you come back out here to the country and see us."

Ben's walker rattled and squeaked all the way down the long ranch-style hall to his bedroom.

"He still acts up a little," Phyllis said. "You know. Brain damage," she whispered, walking back into the kitchen.

Once upon a time, in a galaxy far far away, Ben and I were close, if that's the right word, not just kids who grew up together, but closer even than that, as close as Ben would allow. Especially a couple summers before It, when

I was kind of lost right after high school and so was he. We hung out, him coming up weekends to Dayton, the two of us, almost as a joke, going to that one gay bar they put into the used-to-be Target strip-mall by the interstate. We would get drunk as shit, me commenting whore-like on the men, Ben pretending to be "bi" and macho-- wincing when I got too faggy. He was trying to act like this was all just a phase and that soon he would find a lady and lay lady lay down with her and get married and move into a farmhouse all their own.

Right now, though, it's me sitting in the living room with Ben and Chuck, Phyllis in the kitchen, cleaning off the table, bitching that she has to do everything but not wanting any help. Ben is staring at a plaster-of-Paris statue of a fuzzy-faced bunny on the coffee-table. Chuck is watching *Entertainment Tonight*. I am wanting suddenly and desperately to call Adam who wouldn't be home anyway on a goddamn Friday night. Adam lives with me, but shares his room with his boy-toy now, who shall from now on be called Nameless. The other day, Adam told me, "Me and Nameless are gonna have to get a place of our own," looking all hurt and damaged in the living room of the apartment I was paying for. Adam said that just because I had thrown a little tantrum. I had gotten off work and came home and they were in the shower together and I went into the kitchen and as a joke got a big knife, the biggest goddamn knife, and reenacted the famous *Psycho* shower-scene. I did not kill anyone, however.

You see, I wanted to tell Ben, I am not all there either.

"We are out of water!" Phyllis yells from the kitchen.

To add to the glamour of my visit, The McCordsville Water Treatment Plant had issued a water advisory around four o'clock today, having problems with bacteria in the supply, and people in the surrounding area were told to boil all tap-water for drinking and oral hygiene. "Happens all the time," Chuck told me, arriving home from work. But Phyllis being Phyllis has taken it one step further to include using store-bought water for everything.

She comes into the completely sedate country-decorated living room. "You hear me?" she's talking to Chuck.

"Yeah." He just stays in his lounger, kind of laughing under his breath.

Phyllis laughs, "Well?"

"Well just boil regular tap-water like everybody else," he says.

Phyllis laughs louder. Then stops, like an old-time comedian trying to get more yuks, bugging her eyes out. "No buddy. You get up off your big ass. And you go out and get us some store water. I am not repeat not touching that bacteria. You know that. No."

Chuck stays seated, his under-the-breath laughing growing into a grunt.

This is when I step in. "Ben and me can go get you some." I had to say something. It was like their arguing was my fault, like I had brought the plague of dirty water with me.

Phyllis looked at me, not smiling this time. "You sure?"

"We. Are going," Ben said right off.

Chuck sat back in his La-Z-Boy, knocking the back of the chair into the wall. "Let um go," he said, angry, following that up with his laugh. "Let um fucking go."

Phyllis marched back into the kitchen and came back out with her purse, a white scuffed one, got out her wallet, gave me a $10 bill. "Buy as much as you can with that," she instructed me. It felt like this was her admitting defeat, this was her handing her responsibilities over to me, like the smallest thing had just killed her. "Go on," she said.

Ben had already gotten up using his walker. He stood by the couch, holding onto it, not grinning, his left eye glowing big and dumb in the bright light from the TV. Chuck took off his socks. I crumpled up the $10 bill. Rose. Walked toward the kitchen, hearing the rattling walker behind me, hearing Ben's huffing breath.

Outside, a big orange October moon, and the flat-topped earth, corn-stalks shaved to stubble, the smell of burning leaves. At least now, Ben and I had something to do. I looked at Ben beside my car. He was staring out behind the garage, at a little path that snaked to the other side behind, under a big dead walnut tree next to a stack of fire-wood covered in a blue plastic tarp. All of this was lit by an old pole-light with a rusty basketball goal bolted to it.

The walker sinking slightly into the mud, Ben started

walking toward the path. "Come. On. Come," he said.

I followed, watching his back, his legs as he hobbled across gravel. I flashed to when he was not who he is now, but just a plain old geek, cute, at least to me. Back when we were best friends, he allowed me to suck him off, in his bedroom on this very property. I mean what are the odds? Two queers (except yeah he was "bi") in rural Ohio, one slightly obese, the other skinny, tight-lipped, wanting to escape but not knowing how. Ben truly, in a way, loved Phyllis and Chuck. Loved the silence of the green green grass and the anonymity of radio-towers in the middle of nowhere and going fishing and hunting and mowing long hot acres without his shirt on. Loved the simplicity and exactness of where he was. And just like escaping to Dayton with me, at times, to the bar, to drink but never really do anything, pick up anybody, or even dance. Never talk to me seriously about any of it. His gayness was this private thing he kept away from himself, from them in there in the house right now. Sure he went to the rest-stop on I-75N a few times, he told me, in stalls jerking off with truck-driving angels. But with me, it was like he was allowing me to go down on him as a gift, silent as a gifted actor playing a guilty homo on a prestigious *Hallmark Hall of Fame*.

Now we are back behind the garage, the Death Garage, him gripping the walker. Three pie-pans nailed to little wood planks are jutting out of the weeds back here. I look at Ben's face. He is staring at the pie-pans. After a short while, I get nervous.

"Larry," he says. "Moe," he says. "Curly." Each time
pointing at a separate pie-pan. I try to figure out what he
means. I can't.

He starts laughing. "Dead, man," he says. "Dead." He
laughs, like I should laugh too. So I do, the way a hostage
laughs during a bank heist when ordered. I smile after
I stop. There's the wind-blown silence. There's the pie-
pans rattling softly.

"Mine," he says. But he is not crying. He is grinning.
It's like he gets the joke that is now his life, and when
he turns around to go back I can hear him humming
something almost intelligible. Maybe a Top Ten hit.
Maybe Boys II Men.

The Kroger's is at the bottom of a hill. It's small and
old, like most everything in McCordsville. He is using the
walker of course, going through ancient automatic doors,
walker-wheels squeaking on worn linoleum. A wicked-
witch dummy stands before a display of Dr. Pepper. The
musty smell of an old building mixes in with the smell of
new groceries, fruity and papery. The fat young woman
behind the service desk has dyed blonde hair and a
tanning-booth tan. Her name is Candy. Ben and I both
know her from school.

"Look who's here." Candy waves and smiles. Ben goes
up, but I stay back, having never really known-known her.
Ben talks. Her face gets the strained kind of expression
people have when they listen to people who can't talk fast.
He is talking about the Three Stooges.

"Oh they get me too," she says. "Every time." She
looks over at me. "Hey Mike. How's it going?"

"Just fine."

She smiles. "You still in Dayton?"

"Yeah."

She doesn't know what else to ask, so I nod and walk
on to the water, not wanting to get into it because I
think of the times her and her friends called me a faggot
in the lunch-line. Too much bull-shit to get into at the
McCordsville Kroger's, six years after the fact. I grab a
cart along the way. Then pull ten plastic jugs of water off
the shelves, hearing his goddamn walker crashing down
the aisle. He stops by the cart and motions over to the
liquor bottles which is catty-corner.

"What?" I say, lugging the last water.

"Schnapps," he says.

"What kind?"

"Peach."

"You are gonna drink Peach Schnapps?"

He just blows his lips out in frustration, almost like he is
trying to be cute. "Fuck. Yes."

I laugh. "Okay." I get a bottle of Peach Schnapps.

It's Candy who checks us out, as the other two old-lady
cashiers are busy. She's all extra-crispy and big-chested
in the express lane. I have this feeling that she thinks her
super tan might buy her a ticket out of here. She looks
me directly in the eye, and she knows and I know what
she and her fucking friends thought of me, not really Ben
as Ben stayed in the ag-department for most of his high-

school career, focusing on cows. She runs the jugs of water over the radar pricer, looking back down. Then like she is apologizing, Candy says, "He is the bravest person I think I know. Coming back from that."

I nod. Ben is right next to me, but he is letting her talk about him.

"You want your water in a sack?" Candy goes.

"No thanks," I say. I look at Candy's face. This smile she has is something she learned after high-school, like she took an adult-ed class on how to act once everything is over and you still have to go on.

I load it all up and go, Ben behind me clanging his walker.

"Bye Ben! Bye Mike!" Candy says. I don't look back. "Stay in touch!"

At the ranch, Phyllis helps us get all the water in and starts boiling two gallons of it to make it hot enough to do the stacked pans and dishes. It is 8:30 PM. Chuck already is asleep with *Sabrina the Teenaged Witch* on. Ben and I sit on the couch again, leaving the Schnapps out in the car. I get up almost as soon as I sit down, though, antsy as hell.

Phyllis is wiping down the sink like it is her version of martyrdom. I feel like I have come across her doing something very private, so I smile out of shock and politeness.

"He really is glad you're here," she says.

"Maybe we'll go to the movies tonight," I say.

"Yeah. Get out and blow the stink off." It makes me sad, how hard she is trying to be friendly. "How's your mom doing?"

"Fine," I say. "She's still at Dayton General Hospital." Mom got her LPN license after the divorce. That's why we moved to Dayton too.

I stop there of course, thinking of when Mom comes over to see me now, how I try to hide the fact that I am living with Adam and Nameless, as it would be too perverse to explain, or too embarrassing. So I play it up in front of Mom when she comes, like Adam is my lover, and I am completely, completely happy. I always schedule her visits for when Adam and Nameless are not home. I see her sitting on my couch, looking worried, but smiling. Her dark hair is cut Peter-pan short for convenience, her eyes glass from pulling third trick. She says, "Well looks like you are very happy, Mike."

"Yeah, Mom's fine, doing good," I say, standing there.

"Good." Phyllis keeps wiping.

"Hey," I go. "Who are Larry, Mo and Curly anyway?" Smiling. "Ben took me out behind the garage and showed me these pie-pan tombstones and--"

Phyllis's face goes pale. She stops wiping. "Don't you remember?"

"What?" My smile drops then, as Phyllis turns toward the living room.

"The three kittens," she says, fading it into a whisper.

"What?" I get closer and can see through the kitchen doorway that Chuck must have snored himself awake.

Now he is sitting up.

"The cats were in the garage when he did it," Phyllis whispers loudly. "Remember? Remember? The momma put them inside a big tire in there and nobody knew."

That same stupid smile I have worn all day reignites. I can see in the door-shape Ben's feet on the floor, the walker, Ben's fingers digging into the sofa cushion. I pull back, Phyllis now going over and pouring another gallon jug of store water into another pot on the stove to heat, possibly to wash her hair.

"Oh yeah," she whispers, screwing the lid back on the empty jug. "Oh yeah. Larry, Mo and Curly. He didn't know. I mean it wasn't on purpose. His dad buried them, and it was only like two weeks back when Ben made the markers. His memorial, he said, except he couldn't get the whole word out. Morial, that's what came out. His language skills are all screwed up."

Phyllis walks out to the utility-room where they put recyclables. Yes, I think. Language skills. Phyllis tries to make some order out of the pile of water bottles.

Then Chuck starts yelling. "Did you cut up the goddamn newspaper again for coupons before I get to read it?"

Phyllis yells back from the utility-room: "No I certainly did not!"

In the doorway, Chuck is holding the paper, which has been cut into with scissors. He is super hyper-pissed. Not laughing at all.

"Fucking ruins the paper!" he says, looking at me but talking to himself. "Can't even have a newspaper around this house."

2

The night of his "accident," Ben was driven by ambulance to the hospital where my mom works. The one in McCordsville could not handle brain injuries like his. This was close to the same time Adam was about to move in with me, as well as close to the time I landed my Winn Packaging job. It's like all Ben's tragicness was counterbalanced by my good fortune, right?

I figured Adam moving in with me meant he loved me (he was without Nameless at the time), not that he wanted free-rent. Plus I would be the breadwinner, as Adam made diddley at Helene's as a hairdresser. I would have that power over him, and even though his being a hairstylist sounds stereotypical, Adam is not a fairy, as much as elegant and pouty, with a kind of snotty distance from the real world. Like he is just too good, which only makes me want to somehow conquer his ass, but lovingly, being diligent and loving till the day he caves in.

Or at least that is how the fantasy goes.

At that time, then, I was feeling like Ben's suicide attempt was just this hideous pathetic predicament. I remember thinking what a loser he was, like he can't even kill himself right. Fucking scaredy-cat faggot. I think I might have even said those exact words to Adam, later that same night, as we had drinks at TGIFridays in the mall where his hair-salon was. I was being all melodramatic and upset about my now ex-best-friend doing something so stupid. Seeking Adam's sympathy. Adam nodded, sipping his cocktail. Tan and tall, he had on a stylish ensemble, a white button-down shirt and black jeans, his hair slicked back, his face smooth and sleek.

"Oh I just hate homosexuals who hate themselves," he said and then he sipped again luxuriantly. I watched his lips on the glass.

Anyway, before that, Mom and I met Phyllis and Chuck in the cafeteria at the hospital, where we had coffee and big chocolate-chip cookies prior to Ben's arrival, Phyllis then sporting a hideous perm, Chuck the same in his Armco uniform. Mom was in her white uniform, obese yet pristine, and me I was her slightly obese son who just got a really good factory job. Both me and Mom, I think back now, were acting superior. After all, it was Dayton Memorial Hospital Ben had to come to after their homophobic hatred fucked him up.

"This is a great rehab hospital," Mom said. "Best in the state."

Phyllis and Chuck nodded. They were truly defeated but it was like in their defeat they were relieved. Mom was all proper and shit. She was delicately wording her sentences, sipping her coffee like a teacher. She looked at me with her superior, loving gaze.

Mom said, "He's going to need all our help."

Phyllis said, "Yes."

Chuck said, "You just got to love your kid. That's all." It was like he'd been talking in another imaginary discussion inside his head and that last part slipped out.

"He tried to kill himself," Mom whispered, glaring at her own plump hands on the table-top. "So he is gonna need a reason to live when he recovers. He is going to need parents who don't judge him."

Phyllis took that without saying anything. Chuck got up and got more coffee from the self-serve machine. I pictured Ben one time when I sucked him off. I think it was Christmas Eve when we were both fifteen, right when Mom and Dad were first getting divorced. Ben stood against his bedroom wall like he was about to be executed, smiling though in the light of the aquarium he once kept.

Phyllis got pissed not from anything Mom said in the cafeteria. It was upstairs in the rehab unit, after Ben had arrived. We were all in the waiting room, CNN on the wall TV, waiting till they got all the machinery hooked up in his room.

Mom was preaching about me: "He has a boyfriend, Phyllis. A good job. He is not hating himself."

I was nodding like a back-up singer.

Phyllis turned red. "Stop it."

She got up and walked over to Chuck, who was watching soldiers marching on CNN. They walked toward Ben's room.

Mom laughed. "Come on. Come on. I have to start my shift." Mother and son walked to the elevator. "We can check on Ben later," Mom said. "Come on up with me. We'll talk."

We went up to the premies unit, where she was working at the time. She let me come with her to this glass-surrounded warehouse of incubators, Mom and me walking in front of it toward the nurse's station. Looking in at the incubators, I thought, Jesus Fucking Christ these are the smallest people alive. But I kept my mouth shut. Soon I would be starting my own dead-end job, after quitting my first semester of community college. Soon I would hurl myself full-fledged into my obsession with Adam, my only reason left on earth to live, only heart-ache and heartburn and reenactments of *Psycho* awaiting me.

But for now I was my mom's special queer son in the nursery of premature infants, some blue, some red, some pink, some brown, all so tiny they were like little dreams floating in Plexiglas cubes in their own recording studio inside the hospital. The machines keeping them breathing and their kidneys going and their hearts beating sounded like experimental music no one really wants to hear.

Mom and I walked past them all to the back, where a low-lit nurse's station was. Two or three other nurses were doing paperwork.

"This is Mike, my son," Mom said, putting her purse down on a counter. They did not seem to care. Mom looked at me, "I have a whole shift ahead."

"I know," I said, scanning the eleven incubators, eleven kids. Out there, a skinny red-headed nurse opened one with gloves on, turned over a child the size of a knick-knack.

"I just want you to know, Mike, that I am proud of you," Mom said.

"Thanks." I could not look at her. Right then it hit me. The reason Ben tried to do what he did was he was lonely and I felt kind of triumphant that I was not, or at least I had the ability to pretend I was not.

"I know you're worried about Ben," Mom had tears in her eyes. "But I love you."

I loved her too. I still felt this thrilling dullness inside when she hugged me, though. This was a show she had put on in front of Chuck and Phyllis, and even now in front of the other nurses, this hugging bull-shit was a show, was it not?

But too I melted. And I told Mom how much I loved her.

I left the nursery of incubators to go see Ben a little while later. He was still hooked up to his ventilator. His skin was silvery, his eye-lids like tiny gray clouds. Ben's parents sat off to the side by the window, just silhouettes. In silence, they were allowing me this glimpse at the wet blackness of Ben's hair, his premie-like face, fetal from carbon-monoxide, fetal from trying to push himself out, fetal from having nowhere else left to go.

3

Ben is in his bedroom now, sitting on the bed in the
bright light from an old fashioned, cut-glass light fixture
in the ceiling, the kind moths like. Sitting there in jeans
and a black cowboy kind of dress-shirt, his face calm,
cowboy-boots on his feet, the ever-present walker there
too. I wonder if he sleeps with the thing.

I smell like Safari by Ralph Lauren, the stuff Mom got
me for my birthday. (We went out to Olive Garden, the
waiters and waitresses sang to me, Mom goes, "It's a shame
Adam had to work.") I have on brown corduroys and an
extra-extra-extra-large shirt and loafers, my hair moussed
a little, my face fat and scared and totally plain.

"Ready?" I try to sound encouraging, poking my head
into his room. Posters on the walls have not changed, the
same mix of Garth Brooks Live! and Counting Crows and
Hootie, the same twin-bed with plaid spread, the same
desk with an ancient computer. I step in.

"Yeah. Ready," he says.

I sit down beside him, moving the walker. "I thought
we might go to the 4120—you know the Fort, the bar we
used to go to?"

He does not say anything.

"Okay?" Smiling. It seems like that is all I've been
doing here. "Okay?"

Ben looks at me. His eyes are sleepy. "Fine."

I want to kiss him then. Kiss him for making those pie-pan tombstones, kiss him for still being alive. It is a sudden rush, a twitch inside that can't get out, and it's not about love as much as about fear. I'm afraid that I won't ever be kissed, afraid too that Ben won't ever be kissed either.

Ben and The Walker and me walk down the hall, out to the kitchen. Phyllis escorts us out in her housecoat.

"What you gonna see?" Phyllis asks. We are on the back-porch. She clutches her upper-arms, her ponytail un-rubberbanded, her hair unraveled threads.

"Don't know yet," I say.

Ben just keeps walking with his trusty sidekick. Phyllis nods. Terrified that I will take her damaged boy to an evil place, worried that I won't bring him back. She walks backwards then into the house, talking, "Ben, don't walk fast. You'll trip over that walker. You took your seizure pills right? Good. Be careful."

Her love is about walking backwards into her house. Her love is on the phone with me, "Sure you can come for a visit Mike. Ben misses having people around," like she and Chuck are not people: her love is about forgetting she and Chuck and Ben are people.

Peach Schnapps and Dilantin. Sure I worry. Ben drinks the Schnapps though, downs it, his face stiff from the wonderful flavor. I figure it is all I can give him.

Night-driving is like a dream out here, flat grim little roads folding back, out and around, barbed-wire fences like thousands of stitches after a serious operation, anonymous houses you remember without ever having committed them to memory. I sip too. It is 60 or so miles, and we get on the interstate around 10:30. Ben falls to sleep, the walker sleeping on its side in the backseat in the rearview mirror. Tossing and turning a little with each bump.

I pull into the place finally, the old closed Target strip mall. Lots of cars. I pull up, always uncomfortable coming here, but then where else do I go? To a fucking country-bar with my fellow employees at Winn? That's where I belong right? Not with the Sexy and the Fashion-Conscious and the CK-One-Wearing of Dayton, but with the Lowdown and the Haggard listening to Alan Jackson and Shania Twain, drinking Bud Light, ordering wings. And of course Ben does not belong here either. He belongs at home, saying prayers to the dead kittens, throwing fits, sobbing.

I wake him up though. He starts, the Schnapps bottle dropping.

"Fuck," he says.

"Dreaming?"

"Yes," he snaps.

This is when I get out. I get out and stretch, look around, and then I see Adam and Nameless getting out of Nameless' Tercel. I just stand there, and it hits me that I must have done this on purpose. He and Nameless start walking toward the bar. Meanwhile, groggy and awkward, Ben has gotten out of the passenger side on his own.

Adam and Nameless do not wave. Nameless in leather
pants! Nice hair. Reminds one of George Michael. And
Adam. Once, one time only, he let me kiss him right after
the Gloria Estefan concert I won tickets to off the radio.
Kissed, once, and then me allowing myself to be fucked
over again and again and again until I learned to love it.

"Adam!" I yell.

They stop and point.

I guess this is when I realize Ben has fallen down drunk,
or with a seizure. My fault, my fault. Adam and Nameless
run over. I go and I see Ben on the concrete, one little
bloody place on his forehead from hitting the door maybe
on his way down (goddamn he fell so silently), and I get
the panic, the electrical fear plugged into the socket in my
brain, and I start to cry but then again it's not crying. It's
like a miscarriage.

Ben's face is peaceful on the ground, in seizure-bliss, a
dumb half-shaky tranquility. I bend down and take his
head in my hands, and maybe you are not supposed to lift
people during a seizure or whatever I don't know, but I
am freaked, and Adam goes, I hear Adam go: "Mike, you
want me to call 911?"

"No!" I scream.

Ben's eyes slide open. I think of Jesus in a movie, having
been taken off the cross, Jesus's eyes opening, beautiful
symphonic music playing.

"Just get the hell away," I say, not looking at Adam or at
Nameless, just seeing their shoes on the pavement. Other
shoes too.

Adam goes, "Mike, come on."

Nameless: "I am calling 911."

"No!" That one is a howl.

I look up, and there they are, others gathering. Ben sits up on his own then, like a toddler learning about gravity.

"Home," he says. "Home." Like E.T.

I help Ben up. He slides into the seat. I walk toward Adam. "You can shove 911 up your ass," I say, or maybe just think it.

Adam tells me to stop, Nameless right beside him still. I stop.

"What is wrong with you?" Adam says. "That guy passed out!" His face is full of fear and disbelief. "You need to call an ambulance, Mike. Come on."

I stare at him for a few seconds, into his face, without saying anything.

"Have you lost it?" Nameless says.

I walk backwards to the car, then get in.

The crowd all stand in my headlights, like the end of some serious movie, one nominated for several Oscars, but then it ends up winning zilch.

Phyllis and Chuck are fast asleep. I assist Ben to the bathroom by his bedroom. He slept most of the hour back, and he only puked a little. I was way too afraid to go to a hospital.

I am wiping his forehead as he sits on the toilet. Ben mumbles he is sorry. As I put a Band-Aid on the little cut, I picture him making the three pie-pan grave-markers, picture him walking with them awkwardly outside, planting them into the ground, like finally he has sense enough to do this. Then it is a flash-forward, but then backward too, from here in the bathroom making him better, to the day he did it, the time right before. I see him un-injured, just sitting in his room, plain but not ugly, alone. Then he gets it, like a bird landing on his windowsill, he gets it: hey it's time.

Maybe he has a sore throat, or a long-lost love I don't know about, boy or girl, or a hatefulness so deep it requires immediate action, or maybe Phyllis left a note on the fridge for him to start pulling his weight around here!!!, or maybe he thought about being a little boy forever in a tree-house, his face the size of a dime in a sweet sunny world of after-life tree-houses and butterflies singing Carpenters songs and no reminder of what the world once fucking was, or would always be.

In his room, now bandaged, Ben is fine. I realize I left his walker out in my car. I offer to go get it, but he does not hear me. He slides to the floor. I wonder if I should have woke Phyllis, told her about the seizure or whatever, but it would have gotten ugly I'm sure, and I did not need ugly right then in my life.

Ben pulls out a cardboard box from under his bed, and he says, looking up from it, on his knees: "Shut. The. Door. Lock. It."

I do. Nervous, crazy, knowing something is happening, knowing it. Maybe I should call Mom, tell her he drank Schnapps with his Dilantin, she would not judge, she would--

The lid is off. Inside the box are three photo albums. You know the kind, floral-patterned vinyl covers with FAMILY ALBUM in curlicue gold-leaf. He tells me to take one. I open the cover. Inside are crudely cut-out pictures of men. Just men, preserved under acetate. Men not naked or pornographic, but from Sears catalogs in work-clothes, neckties, underwear, men from Wal-Mart mail supplements in plaid shirts, hands in pockets, staring off into space with masculine skin and crystalline eyes. Men in BVDs cut out from Christmas underwear gift packs. Black and white pictures of men from the newspaper, John F. Kennedy Jr riding a bike in Central park, Al Gore smiling from a porch, an anonymous councilman with a cute mustache. Men hallelujah it's raining men. Nameless, foreign, healthy, not gay not straight, men in regular everyday clothes and in tuxedos. Peirce Brosnan, Tom Cruise, Harrison Ford, the Diet Coke guy. A baseball player spitting out tobacco on the mound, a Marlboro man lighting up at sunrise.

All three are like that. Filled up. He is going to need to buy another album. "This is wonderful," I tell him. "You did this?"

Ben rolls his eyes, sarcastic and sleepy. It hits me then that his life now is about his own nursery of men who do not speak or see or feel or hear or smell or taste, frozen by him, cut out with hands that have gross-motor problems. He waits all day for magazines and supplements and the newspaper to arrive in the U.S. Mail so that he can search, find, preserve.

After a while I stop looking, help him put them away. Ben says, "So?"

"Nice," I say. His room is too bright from the ceiling fixture. I feel dim inside though. I feel like we have been forgotten by the rest of the world, and this is just fine. I don't experience my usual late-night panic, my Adam-induced insomnia. I don't. Ben looks almost like he used to: backwards, kind, and a little confused.

Then I am tucking Ben into bed, kissing him good night, deeply kissing him good night, feeling his hard-on under the plaid spread. Me and my fat-ass climb into his twin bed, after I turn out the lights. We do it.

It's not lovely, God knows, but it means everything. I feel like as we do it we are going back to a time when we were almost the same people, two kids, two stupid boys. I won't go into it anymore though. There's nothing left to say, except to tell you that we don't say a single word. We have a week. A whole week.

This book was made possible
through the generous support of: